Breathing Room

Breathing Room

Marsha Hayles

SQUARE
FISH

Henry Holt and Company
NEW YORK

SQUARE
FISH

An Imprint of Macmillan
175 Fifth Avenue
New York, NY 10010
mackids.com

Library of Congress Cataloging-in-Publication Data
Hayles, Marsha.
Breathing room / Marsha Hayles.
        p.   cm.
"Christy Ottaviano books."
Summary: In 1940, thirteen-year-old Evvy Hoffmeister and her newfound
friends struggle to get well at Loon Lake Sanatorium, where they are being
treated for tuberculosis.
ISBN 978-1-250-03411-3 (paperback) / ISBN 978-1-4668-1603-9 (e-book)
[1. Coming of age—Fiction.   2. Tuberculosis—Fiction.   3. Sick—
Fiction.   4. Hospitals—Fiction.   5. Minnesota—History—20th century—
Fiction.]   I. Title.
PZ7.H3148895Br 2012   [Fic]—dc23   2011034055

Originally published in the United States by
Christy Ottaviano Books/Henry Holt and Company
First Square Fish Edition: 2013
Book designed by April Ward
Square Fish logo designed by Filomena Tuosto

10 9 8 7 6

AR: 5.0 / LEXILE: 800L

To Hannah, Lily, and Nate,
Who helped me make this journey—
Step by step,
Breath by breath

CONTENTS

Breathing
Room

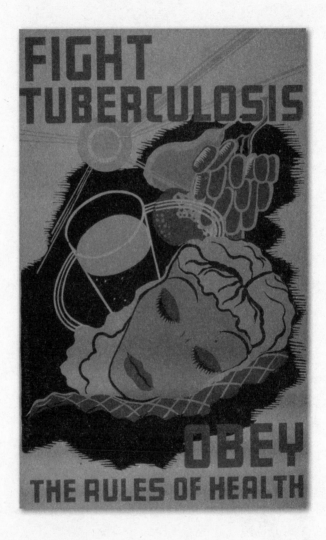

CHAPTER 1

Leaving
(May 1940)

FATHER JERKED THE CAR to the side of the road and stopped. "Are you okay, Evvy?" he asked, turning in his seat to look at me.

I pitched my head back, gasping for air between coughs. *Breathe!* a voice inside me screamed. I dropped the Loon Lake brochure. A blast of heavy, moist air shot up from my lungs and exploded into the handkerchief I'd grabbed and pressed against my lips.

But I could breathe again. "I'm okay, Father," I said, though my voice crackled as if it had just been hatched and never used before. "Really I am."

He sank back down into his seat and grabbed the steering wheel. "Ya got Francy?" he asked, glancing at me in the rearview mirror, worry in his eyes.

I lifted my stuffed bear to show him. Thirteen was too old to be holding on to a teddy bear—at least, that's what Mother thought. I was glad Father didn't feel that way.

"Then get some rest, Puddlejump," Father said, using the nickname he'd given me when I was a little girl. "And don't worry, we'll be there soon." As if that could make me feel any better.

He put the car in gear, and the two of us were off again, driving to Loon Lake—or Loony Lake, as my twin brother, Abe, had already renamed it—a sanatorium where sick and contagious people like me went to get better. At least, that was the hope.

When I knew Father wasn't looking, I opened my hand. The damp handkerchief unfolded just enough so I could see the streaks of blood across it. It wasn't the first time I'd coughed up blood. But I'd never told anybody, not even Abe. I was too afraid. Did this blood mean I was going to die?

WELCOME TO
Loon Lake Sanatorium

LOON LAKE SANATORIUM
LOON LAKE, MINNESOTA

DR. F. H. TOLLERUD, a world-renowned physician and surgeon, heads an outstanding staff at Loon Lake Sanatorium.

Established in 1915, Loon Lake Sanatorium has provided twenty-five years of leadership in the care and treatment of patients suffering from tuberculosis.

LOON LAKE SANATORIUM'S EXTENSIVE CARE OFFERS:

- separate facilities for adults and children
- modern medical treatments
- a highly trained staff of doctors and nurses
- careful patient management
- instruction in proper hygiene and good nutrition
- recuperative therapy
- occupational activities
- a peaceful setting beside Loon Lake

BUT THE *REST* OF THE STORY IS UP TO YOU!
Loon Lake Sanatorium can give you excellent medical care, but
the REST is up to you!

REST means resting your body. You will stay in bed until the doctors determine that you may start a gradual program of activity. Learn to relax and let your body heal.

REST means resting your lungs. Talk only when necessary. Try not to cough or cry.

REST means resting your mind. Keep your thoughts positive. Do not let gloom and doom step into your room! Be a patient patient and you will be well soon.

REST your worries. Your care is in our hands!

Remember you have a contagious disease. Please be considerate of others.
Your journey to good health begins with your arrival at Loon Lake Sanatorium. Welcome!

CHAPTER 2

Loonless Lake

FATHER TOOK THE KEY out of the ignition and reached for his hat. "Well, here we are, Evvy." The sanatorium loomed outside the car window, a giant version of the photo my finger had now smudged on the brochure.

"See any loons?" I asked, as if one might fly by to welcome us.

"No, not yet," he said, walking around to my door.

"How about a lake?"

"Nope, but it's Minnesota, Evvy. One can't be too far away."

I grabbed my stuffed bear and held Father's

hand just long enough to get up on my feet. I didn't want Father going home with my germs.

Father hesitated at the bottom of the stairs leading to the main building. "Maybe I should carry you, Evvy."

"I'm okay, Father, really." I then climbed the first three steps just to show him.

"Hey, wait for me, Puddlejump," he said, as if I'd set off on a race. He paused every few steps to point at flowers in the gardens so I could lean on the railing and rest.

At last, Father opened the building's tall door. *What is that hospital smell? Sick people? Lysol? Bleach?* I felt like my face was being slapped by a damp washcloth.

A young man in a white uniform plunked me into a wheelchair and delivered us to a tall marble counter. We waited a moment, Father's hand on my shoulder, my stuffed bear tucked under my arm. A woman started speaking. I couldn't see the lady's face, just her starched white cap bobbing up and down as she quizzed Father about my "health and family history."

The nurse didn't ask me any questions, and when Father asked her some, I didn't like any of her answers, especially, "Visitors are not allowed at

Loon Lake until authorized by Dr. Tollerud. Your daughter needs to rest, Mr. Hoffmeister. We will decide what is best for her."

The nurse then came out from behind the tall desk. She stood stiff and straight in her white cap and uniform. "I am Nurse Marshall," she said, speaking only to Father. "Dr. Keith and I will be in charge of your daughter's immediate medical care."

At the sight of me, she lifted and tied a white mask to cover her mouth and nose, looking like a robber, not a nurse.

Please don't let her steal me from you, Father!

He tugged at the hat in his hands but couldn't seem to make himself turn toward the door. "Could I have a moment alone with my daughter?"

Nurse Marshall stood up even straighter, answering his request with an icy stare.

"Well, then, thank you, Nurse Marshall." Father nodded politely. "I guess it's time for us to say good-bye, Evvy."

Nurse Marshall took control of my wheelchair and started pushing me away.

"Your mother will miss you," he called. "We all will!" Father was always trying to let me know my mother loved me. I didn't need to be reminded how Abe and Father felt.

I wanted to cry, but not with the nurse so close behind me. Droplets of moisture seemed to weep through my skin—on my hands and chest, even behind my knees—as if everything but my eyes could show how I was really feeling.

Then Nurse Marshall turned a corner and Father was gone. I never did get the chance to tell him good-bye.

LOON LAKE SANATORIUM
CLINICAL RECORD

Patient Number: **22781**

Patient Name: Evelyn Hoffmeister

DOB: 4-9-1927

Admitted: 5-2-1940

Primary Physician: Dr. Harris

Contact: Mr. D.C. Hoffmeister

Assigned Room: 245

Diagnosis: Pulmonary Tuberculosis

Sputum: + +

Exposed to Tuberculosis? If so, by whom?

None from _____ to _____

Status of Family Members: negative

Acid-Fast Smear:

____✓____ Positive

_____ Negative

Acid-Fast Culture:

____✓____ Positive

_____ Negative

Color: pink

Vital Signs:

Temperature ___99°___

Pulse ___92___

Resp. Rate ___18___

Height ___56"___

Weight ___78 lbs___

X-ray:

right upper lobe
infiltrate

Symptoms:

Cough ___✓ productive___

Fever ___✓___

Night Sweats ___no___

Weight Loss ___no___

Status:

____✓____ Active

_____ Inactive

_____ Activity Undetermined

CHAPTER 3

Turning Into
a Patient

NURSE MARSHALL pushed me down a series of corridors, from one building to the next. My legs, which had felt fine in the car, now felt heavy, as if I had thick cough syrup instead of blood running through my veins. I was wheeled past patients resting outside in the fresh air. A few gave me half-hearted smiles as I rolled by, but somehow that just made me feel worse.

One man waved. He was leaning out a window, his lopsided chest crisscrossed with what looked like one of Grandma Hoffmeister's undergarments. *A brassiere? No, a bandage!* A fancy one made of straps that circled under each arm, over his shoulders, and even around his stomach—more like a gun holster than a brassiere. But why did he need it? Would he fall to pieces without it? Would I need one too?

Back inside, hacking, spitting, sputtering coughs rocketed at me from all directions. Doctors and nurses rushed past. With masks over their mouths and noses, they didn't have to try to smile at me.

Then Nurse Marshall rolled me into a large tiled room to be bathed—boiled, actually. I felt like one of Grandma Hoffmeister's cabbages bouncing around in a pot of steaming water. My hair got scrubbed with a smelly green shampoo, my skin was scraped with a bar of soap as big as a brick, and then all of me got dried off with a towel that seemed determined to rub away half my skin and leave the other half red and raw.

I was put in Loon Lake pajamas—white baggy pants and a loose button-up top. "Raising your arms to dress might strain your lungs," Nurse Marshall said in a wooden voice, like someone reading from a manual.

Wait until I tell Abe. Even pajamas can kill you at Loon Lake!

As she cinched me into a white bathrobe, put slippers on my feet, and seated me back in the wheelchair, she continued telling me in the same practiced tone how talking could also damage the lungs and was therefore not allowed at Loon Lake.

My other outfit—the one Mother had carefully chosen and ironed so I would make a good first impression—had been flopped over a metal chair and looked as limp as I felt. Nurse Marshall balled up the clothing, then grabbed Francy by one ear and dropped everything into a metal bin, letting the lid snap shut. "Full of germs," she said.

I couldn't leave Francy behind, not in that cold bin all alone. "Please!" I begged.

"I am not here to coddle you," Nurse Marshall said, pushing my wheelchair out the door. "Kindness will not cure you or anyone at Loon Lake."

Before we'd left Northfield, Father had made me promise not to cry, saying how we'd both have to buck up and be good soldiers. I wondered if he was being a good soldier now too.

One thing I did know for certain: Mother didn't cry this morning. She gave a faint wave, then pulled Abe close as they watched the car back out of the driveway. Was she worried more about me leaving or about Abe getting sick next?

Maybe if Abe had been with me now, I'd have been brave and held back my tears. But I was at Loon Lake all by myself—just Evvy, not half of the Abe and Evvy duo. I felt more lopsided than the man in the window. So when the nurse parked me in a corner and said, "Wait here"—as if I had any choice—I cried, burying my face in the sleeve of a strange, stiff bathrobe instead of the soft, familiar fur of my stuffed bear.

CHAPTER 4

A Gray Picture

NURSE MARSHALL might have noticed my tears had she taken a moment to look at me. Instead, as I wiped my eyes, she backed the wheelchair around and pushed me into an X-ray room. She left, pulling the door closed behind her.

The room looked pretty much the same as where I'd had my X-ray taken back in Northfield.

I looked at all the equipment—the metal knobs and gauges and a tall piece of dark glass. I was glad I didn't need a brassiere yet and would have nothing much to flatten when it came time to press my chest against the glass.

A doctor hurried in, took my X-ray, wheeled me into another room, and zipped a white curtain around me before rushing away. Was I supposed to stay here? Had Nurse Marshall forgotten me already? Had everybody?

I waited. No one came. I kicked at the curtain until my slipper fell off, and I had to scoot out of the chair to retrieve it. I snuck a look at my medical chart—just a bunch of papers stuck between two metal plates. Only one page had any writing on it. I was patient number 22781—that was printed in bigger type than my name. Then I inched my chair over to look out the slender crack between the curtains and saw several screens for viewing X-rays. Dr. Harris's office only had one.

Five minutes passed, if I could believe the clock on the wall. Then the door swished open and footsteps scuffed along the shiny floor.

I peeked around the curtain. A doctor stood across the room—not the older one who took my X-ray but a younger one with a pair of glasses on his nose and another pair sticking out of the pocket of his white coat. His brown hair puffed out in all directions, and his face seemed as tired and rumpled as his clothes—like he'd slept with the chickens, Father would say.

He lifted a big sheet of floppy paper and clipped it to a screen. A grayish white picture appeared.

Could that be my X-ray, the one they just took?

Probably not, unless they could develop film much faster here than Dr. Harris could back home.

I tilted my head the way the doctor did, then tapped my own chest to match what I felt with what I was seeing. The T across the top must be the collarbones, the white blob at the bottom the stomach.

But what about the lungs? Had they disappeared? Could tuberculosis do that? I blinked. This time I saw shadows in and around the ribs. Those must be the lungs—just full of air and hard to see, like gray ghosts floating around inside a cage.

The door opened again. At the sight of Nurse Marshall I shut my eyes, but I still listened.

"Dr. Keith, excuse me. I didn't know you were using this room. I believe my patient—"

"Nurse Marshall, look at this."

Did she say Dr. Keith? Wasn't that the name of my new doctor?

The two started speaking in what sounded like a foreign language. I recognized only a few words—"cavitation" and "lobe"—words I'd heard Dr. Harris use before.

A cough prickled loose in my chest and started to scratch its way up my throat. *Not now!* I pressed my face into my sleeve—still damp from my tears. My shoulders twitched forward, and I coughed into my thick robe.

Had they heard me? I waited. No one came. They kept right on talking. Coughs must be as common here as snowflakes in winter: hardly worth noticing.

"Dr. Keith, certainly you are far more qualified than I am to make such an assessment."

"Yes, but I thought since she's one of yours, Nurse Marshall, you might be able to—to talk to her." Dr. Keith's voice sagged with each word. "Encourage her to rest more. She works too hard."

"Unfortunately, Doctor," Nurse Marshall said with an impatient firmness, "her nature is as stubborn as her disease."

I heard a single click—the doctor must have been turning off the screen for viewing the X-ray—and then a sigh.

Who are they talking about? And why does the doctor sound so sad? I'd never thought about a doctor being worried. Dr. Harris always acted like he'd seen everything—from Abe's bad case of the chicken pox to the

oozing boil Grandma once got on her wrist. I wondered why this doctor asked Nurse Marshall what
she thought. Wasn't he the doctor?

My head hurt with questions. Really, all of me
hurt. Worse than ever before. I had to close my eyes.
Trying to stay alive at Loon Lake felt like it was killing me already.

CHAPTER 5

The Others

"WAKE UP."

I opened my eyes, confused for a moment until I realized I must have fallen asleep after the X-ray. Abe would rib me if he knew I could doze off like that while sitting straight up. Next I'd probably start snoring.

Nurse Marshall said nothing else as she propped

open a door with her hip, then swung my chair around and into what felt like a wall of sunshine. I squinted, my head still hurting, until I could make out the large opened windows and a door ahead of me. My eyes adjusted more, and I saw beds—two empty ones on my left and three with girls in them on my right. This must be my room— our room, I guessed.

"Your bed, Evelyn," Nurse Marshall told me, saying my name for the first time. But she pronounced it all wrong, like she was saying *Evil-in*. "At the present time, Evil-in, you will share this room with three others." She prepared the bed and nodded in the direction of each girl as she said their names.

"Pearl" was sitting up. She patted her curled, light brown hair, then waved a movie magazine in my direction to say hello. "Beverly" was next. She had long blond braids flanking a face as round and pale as a sugar cookie. She lifted her head off the pillow to smile at me. The third girl, "Dena," started coughing, so all I could see was a shake of dark, straggly hair and a fist covering a mouth.

"Control your cough, Dena," Nurse Marshall said, pausing at the empty bed next to mine. She lifted me up onto a bed sheet that was stiff as paper, then folded the cover of a heavy blanket over me. I felt like I was being pressed inside a book.

"My name's Evvy," I said to the ceiling. "It rhymes with Chevy, the car."

"No talking!"

I didn't care if Nurse Marshall yelled at me or not. I couldn't have these girls calling me by the wrong name.

"Evvy and her Chevy," the girl with straggly hair said from across the room. She dropped her hand from her mouth to point at me, then at the wheelchair.

"Enough, Dena!" Nurse Marshall said, the heels of her oxfords pecking at the floor as she moved about the room. Did she have to yell all the time? We weren't talking that much, just a few words.

I stared at the dull ceiling. Not even a crack or splotch for my mind to pick at like a scab—just plain white. White above me, white below me, white on all sides. I tipped my head to look to my left: the empty bed. To the right: two doors—one I'd just come through, and the other? Maybe a closet or a bathroom. I didn't want to find out—not yet. A little mystery was better than a lot of boring.

I discovered that my body seemed to have a secret life of its own. My fingers and toes stretched and twitched without my command. Tiny bubbles of sweat squeezed out all over me. My ribs seemed to grind and tighten just before a stormy cough blew up and out of my chest. Then a more familiar feeling demanded my attention. I needed to go to the bathroom. Now. But if I couldn't talk, how could I ask to get up? And would I even be allowed?

Abe had overheard Grandma Hoffmeister say I would probably be using a bedpan. "Maybe it'll look like one of Grandma's cake pans!" he'd said. I'd laughed along with him, too embarrassed even to ask what a bedpan looked like or how it worked. Now I wished I had.

I tried raising my hand like we did at school. Nurse Marshall was too busy to notice, shaking down a thermometer, then jamming it in my mouth. I'd have to wait ten minutes, unless temperatures got taken faster here than in Dr. Harris's office.

I crossed my ankles.

No help.

I tightened my muscles and tried to zip my body shut.

Can't the nurse tell what's wrong?

I squirmed to give her a hint.

She checked her watch, not me.

Please just take the thermometer out of my mouth!

My brain jumped into action, making up a song that bounced around inside my head: *Evvy had a little pan, little pan, little pan. Evvy had a little pan and surely had to go.*

At last Nurse Marshall tapped her watch and slid

the thermometer out of my mouth. The word "bath-room" spilled out of me.

Nurse Marshall brought over the bedpan. It was oval—like a small, squashed toilet seat made out of metal. She pulled the curtain around my bed, had me bend my knees up like two snowy mountains under the sheet, and tipped me just enough to slip the cold bedpan like an icy shovel under my bottom. I did my splattery, noisy business, embarrassed that everyone could hear. She pressed tissue into my hand so that I could wipe myself. *Will I always be able to do that? If I get too sick, will that be her job?* I was just glad that at least this time I didn't have to do anything that would stink up the room.

My head dropped back to the pillow, and patient 22781 fell sound asleep.

CHAPTER 6

The Land of Rules

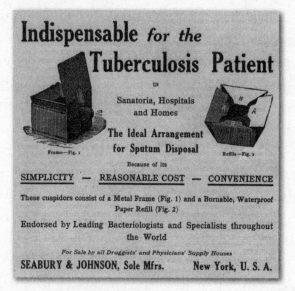

Indispensable *for the* Tuberculosis Patient

IN

Sanatoria, Hospitals
and Homes

The Ideal Arrangement
for Sputum Disposal

Frame—Fig. 1   Refills—Fig. 2

Because of its

SIMPLICITY — REASONABLE COST — CONVENIENCE

These cuspidors consist of a Metal Frame (Fig. 1) and a Burnable, Waterproof
Paper Refill (Fig. 2)

Endorsed by Leading Bacteriologists and Specialists throughout
the World

For Sale by all Druggists' and Physicians' Supply Houses

SEABURY & JOHNSON, Sole Mfrs.   New York, U. S. A.

"SPIT," A VOICE ORDERED.

My eyelids felt glued shut.

"We need to check your sputum," the voice said, this time sounding more insistent.

One eye unsealed. The other eye opened to see a cup jammed in front of my face. A strange cup. More square than round, with a metal lid flapped open and a paper liner inside.

"Expectorate, Evil-in," the voice ordered again.

I looked around at the other girls. They were all spitting into little cups.

I leaned forward and coughed something thick and yellowish that landed with a wet thud onto the bottom of the tin.

Once the hock-hocking stopped and the spitting was done, cup lids were closed, and we each used a paper hankie to wipe our mouths. The other girls placed their soiled mouth wipes into the bag by their beds. I did the same, then dropped my head back to my pillow.

"I see we're feeling better," Nurse Marshall said as she gathered the cups. At first I thought she was talking about all the girls in the room—what were their names again?—but then I realized her eyes focused just on me.

"You spiked a fever, Evil-in," Nurse Marshall said. "No matter how carefully we try to instruct families in advance, new patients invariably arrive here exhausted. Dr. Keith insisted I allow you to sleep. But now you must eat."

The back of my neck was slick with moisture, and my legs and arms felt limp and jittery at the same time. Worse, my mouth had a terrible taste, as if I'd eaten a fat slug. But at least I could remember their names now—Pearl, Beverly, and Dena.

The three were allowed to sit up and feed themselves off tray tables positioned over their beds. Not me. Nurse Marshall propped me up on pillows, just high enough so I could swallow. At least, I hoped I could. She then spooned me my first meal.

"Drink your milk slowly," Nurse Marshall cautioned as she slipped the straw into my mouth. "Gulping encourages gas."

"Good to know something gets encouraged around here," a voice across the room grumbled.

"Dena!" Nurse Marshall snapped without turning to look at the girl.

I glanced around between bites of boiled egg to see which one Dena was—oh, the one with straggly dark hair. Her bed was directly opposite mine. She ignored me and Nurse Marshall's reprimand.

How old were these girls? Were any of them thirteen like me, or were they all older? I certainly felt like the baby in the room with Nurse Marshall feeding me this way.

Beverly, the one with the blond braids, put down her glass and turned to look out the window. Could she see anything out there? The lake, a bird, a mosquito—anything? My brain felt hungrier than my stomach.

Then Pearl got my attention just by the careful way she placed her movie magazine down on her bedside table. I bet she was the oldest—at least she acted the most grown-up. I watched as she lifted her egg cup and moved it like a chess piece into playing position. She held the egg with one hand, then with the other tap, tap, tapped the eggshell at the top to make a small opening before scooping out spoonfuls of soft-boiled egg. In between bites, she painted butter on the toast, then ate the bread—crusts and all. I had never seen anyone make such a show of eating. When she finished, she pressed her napkin against her lips and let it fall the way I imagined a queen would drop the train of her gown.

By then, Beverly and Dena were done too, though with a quick lift of my head I could see some food left on Dena's tray.

Nurse Marshall did as well. "A healthy, rich diet is essential if you are to defeat your illness. Those who squander food squander their health!" She emphasized her point by feeding me drippy chunks of grapefruit and spoonfuls of oatmeal. I chewed and swallowed and chewed some more, and felt like a clogged drain about to overflow. But I ate everything.

Nurse Marshall gathered the dishes from the other girls' tables and loaded them onto a cart, telling me more rules as she worked. "No talking, no laughing, no unnecessary activity. Control your coughs or they will control you. Your work here, Evil-in, is to rest and recover. This is not summer camp. You are here not to make friends but to defeat your disease."

Her long list of Loon Lake rules felt like the hardest thing to swallow.

CHAPTER 7

Smelly Stuff

"Bottled   Sunlight"

Extra rich in "sun-
shine vitamin" D. Pos-
sesses a fine, wholesome
flavour.

I LOOKED STRAIGHT UP into Dr. Keith's face—
well, actually, up his nose. Did all doctors have so
much hair in their nostrils?

"Roll onto your side, please, so I can listen to
your lungs."

I felt the cold metal of the stethoscope play

hopscotch across my back. I thought of all the questions I wanted to ask. Like, why did I feel so twitchy and jumpy? My fingers tapped atop my sheets; my toes wiggled all day under the covers. Was this because I was sick, or did I just have a case of the fidgets, as Mother called them? Why did I wake up with my pajama top sticking to my skin? And when would I earn my first privilege, like being allowed to get mail or sit up and read a book?

But after four days at Loon Lake, the one thing I'd learned is that no one seemed to ask doctors or nurses questions. Maybe they were too busy to give us answers. Or maybe, because we were kids, no one would tell us the truth anyway.

Still, couldn't someone at least give me a hint or two about what to expect at this place? Or maybe ask how I was feeling, or tell me why Dr. Keith looked like he'd stirred rather than combed his hair, or why Nurse Marshall always acted liked she'd just swallowed a box of starch?

Dr. Keith whirled out of the room, and Nurse Marshall returned. She stepped over to a locked metal cabinet, opened it, and brought out a brown glass bottle with a picture of a fish on it.

"Ah, shoot," Dena said in a low voice.

Nurse Marshall arched an eyebrow in Dena's

direction, then took a large spoon from each girl's tray and filled it with a yellowish fluid from the bottle.

Dena pinched her nose to down the smelly stuff, Beverly closed her eyes and strained as if swallowing a balled-up sock, and Pearl—forgetting for the moment to be a queen—drank sloppy gulps of orange juice to flush the rotten taste out of her mouth. All three watched to see how I'd handle my first taste of this stuff.

Only, it wasn't. I'd tasted it many times before, thanks to Grandma Hoffmeister.

She would make us take cod-liver oil whenever she stayed with us, though we always complained. Then, as news of the war in Europe came in, she read that supplies of cod-liver oil were running low in England. "Zis war—bad for children, bad for everyone!" She smacked her rolling pin down hard on her strudel dough, exploding a cloud of flour onto her apron and face. Abe and I took our cod-liver oil without saying a word. When we had finished, she lifted the clean corner of her apron to wipe her cheeks, then said with a sheepish smile, "Look how I make a snow grandma instead of apple strudel!"

I missed my snow grandmother now as Nurse Marshall pushed the spoon between my lips. I didn't flinch or gag as I swallowed the fishy oil, though no one seemed to appreciate my skill.

Maybe I should have pretended to hate the cod-liver oil, just to fit in. Abe would have laughed and smacked me on the back if I'd shown him up, then challenged me to some other contest. We competed but cheered each other on.

Here at Loon Lake, it looked like I was a team of one.

CHAPTER 8

Going Home

"DO YOU THINK the new girl's ever going to talk? I just know she'll like me."

"You don't know anything, Pearl. Let her sleep."

The girls had been off to Activity, though what that meant exactly and how active anything around here could be, I didn't know. But at least it seemed to include some talking. I listened but kept my eyes closed, pretending to be asleep.

"Oh, be quiet, Dena. If Mr. Clark Gable himself walked in this door, you'd find something rude to say to him. You have no manners."

"And you have no brains, Pearl. No movie star like Clark Gable would ever set foot in a place like this."

I let the two voices bounce back and forth in my head, the way I did in bed at home when my parents called to each other from different rooms in the house.

"He might for charity, Dena!"

"Oh, that'd be great, Pearl. To have famous people feeling sorry for us."

A third voice entered the conversation now. "Quiet, please, both of you. She doesn't need to hear you two squabbling with each other."

"Ah, quit playing mother hen, Beverly. Look, Evvy's not even awake."

Someone had just said my name—and said it right. I opened my eyes. Dena was looking down at me, her bright eyes full of interest and irritation, as if I were the last crumb in the cookie jar. She turned away. "Sleeping Beauty's awake."

I blinked, not sure what to say. Pearl glanced in

my direction, then grumbled to Beverly, "Dena woke her up, not me!"

Beverly slowed as she walked by, smiled, and touched my blanket, as if that's how you'd say hello at the sanatorium.

"Is there someone in that bed?" I asked, pointing to the empty one next to mine.

Beverly twisted the end of one of her braids, her smile fading. "You're in what used to be Shirley's bed. She aged up to the women's ward—"

"I'm the next one to turn sixteen," Pearl interrupted. "But I should be leaving Loon Lake before then." She stepped back into bed, letting her sheets flounce and flutter around her.

Dena looked toward the empty bed. "Or going home like Marianne."

"You know that wouldn't have happened," Pearl protested, "if Marianne had let them do a pneumo."

"Please, you two—" Beverly coughed into a paper handkerchief, then crumpled it up and put it into the brown bag by her bed.

"A pnuemo?" I asked.

"The doctors push air into your chest so your lung goes flat and can rest," Dena explained. "It's just another stupid treatment."

"No, it's not stupid!" Pearl snapped back. "A

pneumothorax can make all the difference! That's why I want one."

Dena laughed. "It's all a lot of hot air. It hasn't done anything for me."

Pearl sat up straighter in her bed. "That's because of your attitude, Dena. If you did just one thing recommended in the *Loon Lake Booster*, you'd be discharged in no time. Look at me—why, I can even walk to the lake now!"

Dena let her dark, stringy hair flop down in front of her face, then aimed her eyes in Pearl's direction. "Why don't you just jump in it next time, Pearl."

I'd never heard two people bicker like this before. I could see why Beverly looked out the window so much, though I didn't know how she managed to smile at all, living with these two.

"So, can we talk around here or not?" I asked.

Beverly sighed. "We really shouldn't, Evvy, but we do. Usually when the staff is busy—like right now, before they bring us dinner."

"Can I ask another question?"

Beverly nodded. "Just don't ask them all today. And if Dena points her finger at you, stop talking. She always seems to know when someone's coming."

"Especially Old Eagle Eye," Dena said with a smirk.

"Really, Dena, there's no need to call Nurse Marshall a name," Pearl said.

"It's not a bad name. I coulda called her an old bat or something worse—"

The two started arguing again, though I had to side with Dena on this point. Nurse Marshall did have an eagle eye, and she wasn't exactly young either.

But I didn't want to talk about her. I had too many other questions to ask. I cleared my throat. No one paid any attention. I waved my hand. Still no one noticed. Finally, in desperation, I lifted my legs from under my covers and swung them around in the air.

That got their eyes on me. "Could I ask a question now?"

Beverly smiled and nodded. "Please do."

I let my legs drop back to the bed. "Okay. What do they do with our spit?"

Dena chuckled, though not in a friendly way. "Spit's called sputum here, Evvy. We cough some up into those sputum cups, and the docs look at it under a microscope to see if there are still TB germs swimming around in there."

I wished Dena hadn't used the word "swimming." I imagined germs diving and kicking around in my lungs like squirmy little versions of Abe and me swimming in Lake Pepin last summer.

Pearl changed that picture fast. "Oh, those poor little piggies!"

How did pigs fit in to all this?

"You don't care about those pigs, Pearl, and you know it," Dena sniped.

"I do too care," Pearl whined. "It's just so sad."

"They call our germs pigs?" I asked.

Dena propped herself up on her elbows. "Nah. But every so often, the doctors stick our germs into a guinea pig. If the pig lives, you're negative for active TB. You might get to leave this place. That doesn't happen much. We like to kill guinea pigs around here."

Beverly gave Dena a weary look. "We don't kill the pigs, Dena, our disease does."

"Well, my next guinea pig will live. I'm certain of it," Pearl said. "I can feel myself getting better every day."

"We all are." Beverly spoke in such a soothing tone, I almost expected her to read us a bedtime story next.

Then something else clicked in my mind. "A negative result would be good, but the opposite . . . Is that what the plus sign on my chart means? That my spi—my sputum—is still positive?"

"That's right. You're as sharp as a knife, Evvy," Dena said in such a gruff way that I didn't know if I should feel complimented or not.

So I looked at Beverly with my next question. "Would a negative sign mean I'm cured?"

Beverly hesitated. "Not exactly. That means your body has learned to fight off the TB by building walls around it."

"In other words, Evvy, sick or well, you're a bug for life." Dena didn't seem to mind calling us bugs, but I didn't like it. Just because I had TB didn't mean I'd sprouted antennae and needed to be swatted.

I tried switching topics. "Didn't you say that girl Marianne went home?"

More uncomfortable quiet.

Finally Beverly looked over at me, her eyes glistening. "She didn't go home, not the way you're thinking, Evvy. When people in the sanatorium say someone's going home, what they mean is—"

Her voice faltered, and Dena jumped in. "What they mean is that the person croaked. Sold the farm, rode the last train, swallowed the last pill, killed their last pig, breathed their last breath, dropped doorknob dead. You get it?"

Dena's words came at me like gunshots and filled my eyes with tears.

"Look, Dena," Pearl said, "you made her cry."

Beverly whispered, "I'm sorry, Evvy."

But Dena didn't apologize. "Lying to Evvy won't do her any favors. She might as well know the truth. People die at Loon Lake all the time."

CHAPTER 9

A Different Tune

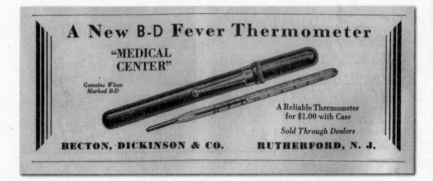

A New B-D Fever Thermometer

"MEDICAL CENTER"

Genuine When Marked B-D

A Reliable Thermometer for $1.00 with Case

Sold Through Dealers

BECTON, DICKINSON & CO.   RUTHERFORD, N. J.

I COULDN'T SHAKE Dena's words, especially when the room got dark in the evening. I didn't believe in ghosts, but I also didn't *not* believe in them. Every puff of air felt like it could be the dead girl's last breath whispering to me. Abe might think I was acting like a ninny, but he'd never tried sleeping in a room where someone had died. If he had, he might not be so brave either.

Still, I didn't mean to gasp when the night nurse

appeared by my bed, flashlight in hand, to check on us.

"Oh, I startled you," she said. "Sorry. Here I've gone and scared you, and we haven't even met each other yet. I'm Nurse Gunderson."

I squeaked out my name, then said hello.

Her lively blue eyes smiled at me from above her white mask.

"Well, welcome, Evvy," she said. She put her hand atop mine. It felt light and warm and, best of all, unhurried. No quick moves to check my pulse or reach for a thermometer or straighten my pillow. "I'm happy to be taking care of you."

"I'm glad too," I said, even happier because she didn't shush me when I spoke.

Her blond hair was pinned up under her nurse's cap, but little tufts snuck loose and, unlike anything else at Loon Lake, looked soft to the touch.

"Now I need to take your temperature, Evvy."

Could she tell how much I hated the long wait it took to get an accurate temperature? She must have, because she leaned over and said, "Pick a song, Evvy, and sing it in your head. We'll have your temperature done in no time."

I thought for a second, then whispered, "In My Merry Oldsmobile." Nurse Gunderson started to hum the melody as she slipped the thermometer into my mouth. Soon I was riding along with Lucille and her suitor in their merry Oldsmobile.

I was glad Nurse Gunderson couldn't actually hear me sing. I could hardly carry a tune, despite my mother being a music teacher. But sometimes on a car trip with the windows wide open, I'd join in and sing loudly, especially my favorite lines:

> *Come away with me, Lucille*
> *In my merry Oldsmobile*
> *Down the road of life we'll fly*
> *Automo-bubbling, you and I.*

For a moment now with my eyes closed, I could almost hear Abe's clear voice carrying the melody as Mother added her high harmonies and Father bellowed through the low notes.

Nurse Gunderson popped the thermometer out of my mouth just as the happy couple drove off to the church to get married.

"Evvy," Nurse Gunderson leaned in close to say, "I think I almost heard some 'automo-bubbling' coming right out your ears!"

I grinned, then pretended to turn a steering wheel over the road of my rumpled blanket. She smiled, then tucked me in and went to check on the others.

For the first time since I'd arrived, I felt my body relax and sink comfortably into the bed. Maybe, with Nurse Gunderson's help, I really could rest and get better here.

LOON LAKE SANATORIUM
SCHEDULE

7:00	Rising Bell
7:15	Temperature and Pulse Taken, Sputum Check
8:00	Breakfast
9:00	Doctor Visits
9:30	Morning Milk
9:45	Rest, Class, or Activity Period as Ordered
11:30	Activity Period Ends
12:00	Dinner and Mail
1:30	Cure Hour
3:30	Snack
4:00	Rest or Activity Period
6:00	Supper
7:00	Rest or Activity as Ordered
8:00	Take Temperature
8:30	Hot Milk or Cocoa
9:00	Lights Out

CHAPTER 10

The Routine

(June 1940)

I SETTLED IN TO the weary Loon Lake routine. I drank glass after glass of milk until I imagined my insides looking as white as a Minnesota winter. I tried to sleep through Nurse Marshall by day and stay awake for Nurse Gunderson at night. I soon learned to recognize my roommates more by their coughs than their voices.

Each afternoon was burdened with a long Cure Hour—a false name if ever there was one. We weren't cured, and it lasted two hours. During that time, talking was strictly prohibited. All the girls except Dena seemed to sleep or at least close their eyes. She remained wide awake, as if on guard duty. Nurse

Marshall liked to point out that even people in the nearby town kept quiet during Cure Hour so we at Loon Lake could rest.

I didn't see any signs that all this rest was helping. I still coughed sputum thick as a raw oyster into the metal cup every morning, I still had a temperature each afternoon, my heart still seemed to quiver instead of beat, and I could still see the plus mark on my medical chart. And I hadn't earned the first privilege yet of getting mail.

"News from home often proves upsetting for our new patients," Nurse Marshall had explained, as if not hearing from home made things any easier.

Beverly got so many letters that she had to tie them up in a stack with string. I wanted to steal one of hers—a hand-me-down letter would have been better than none at all. Once, Dena caught me eyeing Beverly's notes from home. "In a few weeks, Evvy, they'll act like you're getting better and give you mail privileges."

A few weeks? I wanted to hear from my family now! Did Abe get his snazzy new band uniform yet? Had Father dug out the stubborn rhubarb patch in the backyard? Was Grandma still baking cakes and strudels, even without me there to eat them? I tried not to think about Mother. She was probably so busy directing her music groups that she didn't make time to miss me.

Over that whole long first month, I felt gloomy inside and out. Probably the only thing I had in common with the other girls—besides our illness—was that we all liked Nurse Gunderson. And for good reason. She knew Pearl had read and reread *Gone with the Wind* but hadn't been able to see the movie yet. So Nurse Gunderson brought in an old issue of *Life* magazine, full of pictures from the movie's opening in Atlanta, for Pearl to read and keep.

Like Beverly, Nurse Gunderson had grown up on a farm with a big family, so the two would sometimes compare notes on the care of something called pullets, which—I learned by eavesdropping—were young hens.

Dena was a tougher case to charm. I once woke up and saw Nurse Gunderson patting Dena's shoulder, saying something about someone being safe now. I didn't know what they were talking about, but I was surprised to see Dena let anyone get that close.

And Nurse Gunderson was the only staff member who called me Evvy. I would have liked her for that alone.

But even with Nurse Gunderson around, Loon Lake was a sad place, especially late at night, without my bear Francy, alone in my miserable thoughts. If Abe and I always did everything together, why didn't he get sick too? How come he was healthy and at home, and I was sick and stuck here? It just wasn't fair. On my worst nights, I wished Abe had gotten TB too.

I hated those thoughts the most, afraid maybe I really was turning into "Evil-in."

HITLER BARES PLANS FOR FUTURE WORLD ORDER

The dispatch which follows is, on its face, packed with propaganda. It is, at the same time, an historic document and is published for that reason.

By KARL H. VON WIEGAND

Noted foreign correspondent for 25 years, an outstanding American political observer in Europe and the far east.

Copyright 1940, reproduction in whole or in part forbidden.

WITH the German Armies Nearing Paris, June 13 — "The Americas to Americans, Europe to Europeans."

This reciprocal basis Monroe doctrine, mutually observed, declared Adolf Hitler to me today, not only would insure peace for all times between the old and the new worlds, but would be a most ideal foundation for peace throughout the whole world.

In caustic language, with scorn and indignation, he denounced "the lies" that he has or ever had in "dream or thought" played with the faintest idea of interfering in the western hemisphere by any manner or means.

He characterized America's fears of him or Germany as most flattering but "childish and grotesque."

and the whole idea of the possibility of the invasion of the United States from Europe by sea, air or the "mythical fifth column" as "stupid and fantastic."

With his great German war machine, whose amazing perfection of organization, strength, strategical and tactical leadership has startled the world, now on the edge of Paris, Hitler told me he had no intention of attacking the beautiful French capital if it "remains an open city like Brussels."

Vehemently, the Fuehrer denied he ever had or ever now has as a war aim the "smashing of the British

empire." But with bitter anger, he declared "I will destroy those men who are destroying that empire."

He spoke warmly of Premier Mussolini and welcomed Italy's entrance in the "comradeship of arms."

A plane picked me up in the airport of a city where sirens, the deep baying of anti-aircraft guns and dull explosions which sounded like bombs had awakened me after midnight. I was so tired that I did not care what happened and I went to sleep again in the plane.

(Continued on Page 4, Column 2)

Minneapolis Morning Tribune
A MINNEAPOLIS INSTITUTION SINCE 1867

Seventy-Fourth Year.   No. 31.   Thirty-two Pages   MINNEAPOLIS, MINN., FRIDAY, JUNE 14, 1940.   • • •   Three Cents in Minneapolis

---

AMBASSADOR BULLITT REPORTS:

NAZI TROOPS IN PARIS

Reynaud Begs U. S. For Quick Aid to France

Palmersten's Evidence Used Against Him

Testimony Given for Weisman Admitted Over Protest

UNCONSTITUTIONAL, DEFENSE CHARGES

Betty Ryan Testifies She Gave Defendant $300 on Request

At Palmersten's own words, spoken from the witness stand in the recent Davis-Weisman "vice pay-off" trial, were entered against him by the prosecution in its own duly-neglect trial before District Judge E. A. Montgomery yesterday.

Defense attorneys sought to bar the words as a violation of the constitutional rights of the former special agent head, but were over-ruled by the court. They tried to show the scope of offering other testimony he had given before. They were blocked by court ruling.

Developments of Day

The prosecution resorted to the broadcast case record in a day of developments that included:

Testimony of Betty (Frenchy)

OLD FLAG IN NEW AGE

Flag that will have more than ordinary significance today is the home of Mr. and Mrs. Otto Madsen, 2614 Thirty-third avenue north, for Jerome, left, and Donald Steffen are the third generation in their family to affirm allegiance by this 13-star flag which was made when there were only 13 United States. The flag was handed down to their mother by her father, Paul McWhorter, who ...

Britain Makes New Pledge of War to Finish

Assures France She Will Share in Cost of Reparations

QUICK RESPONSE MADE TO REYNAUD

London Promises Utmost to Liberte Enslaved Nations

London, June 14.— (P)— Great Britain today renewed her pledge "to continue the struggle at all costs in France, in the island, upon the seas and in the air wherever it may lead us."

This pledge was made shortly after Premier Reynaud of France had said there was "no armor" in continued resistance unless there was a "repeated" democratic victory in sight.

Will Continue Fight

Great Britain will continue to give the utmost aid in her power, said the British government's message to France.

"We shall never turn from the conflict until France stands safe and secure in all her greatness," it said, and all the wronged states and nations of enslaved states and nations ...

AT A GLANCE

WASHINGTON — Ambassador Bullitt sends word Germans are in Paris; Senate immediately approved $50,000,000 fund for war refugees.

TOURS, FRANCE— Reynaud in "now and then" appeal to Roosevelt for "clouds of airplanes" from United States as French seeks desperate stand, Paris declared open city in aim to save it from destruction; French position desperate to bitter end.

BERLIN—High command says air force and navy destroyed 142 Allied warships in Scandinavian campaign.

ROME—Italy fights off air attack; Badoglio reports new men and material in aid France; air fight over Suez not yet fully decided in Italy's favor as Italian army will punch soon.

LONDON—British spend more men and material to aid France; repeal air force strikes at Italy by land and sea; Italian planes bomb Malta again.

ANKARA — Turkey concludes trade pact with Germany but says Allies depend in Turkish press alerts still conveys against Italy.

MOSCOW—Russia appoints ambassador to Rumania in move to restore diplomatic relations.

'Final' Appeal Made to F. R. For Airplanes

'We Wait With Hope in Our Hearts,' Premier Tells U. S.

URGES CRAFT BE SENT 'IN CLOUDS'

Americans Challenged to Declare Themselves 'Against Nazis

(Text of Appeal on page 11)

Tours, France, June 13.—(P)— Premier Paul Reynaud made a "final" appeal tonight to President Roosevelt for "clouds" of aircraft and challenged Americans to "declare themselves against Nazi Germany."

"We know what a high place ideals hold in the life of the great American people," he said in a broadcast to the country while the German bombers struck down on both sides of Paris.

"Will they hesitate yet to declare themselves against that Germany?

Wants 'Clouds of Planes'

In summoning his utmost plea to Mr. Roosevelt for aid—the first, asking aid and short of an expeditionary force having been made public today—the premier declared

'Inside the Gates' Of Vacated City, Washington Told

Pounding Nazi Armies Turn Drive Toward Tours—Britain Makes Supreme Effort to Turn Tide

By Associated Press

The German army is "inside the gates of Paris," Ambassador William C. Bullitt informed the state department in Washington early today.

"The city was quiet," Bullitt's message said. He had telephoned Ambassador Anthony J. Drexel Biddle, United States envoy to the Polish government now at Tours, France.

Biddle relayed the message to Washington.

Bullitt, who has remained at his post in Paris, sent the notification at 7 p. m. Minneapolis time, but it was nearly midnight before Biddle got word to the state department.

(In London a spokesman for the French embassy said at 1 a. m. Minneapolis time today, that he had no confirmation of the report that the German army was inside the gates of Paris.)

Telephone communication from London to Paris was said by telephone officials to be "not closed," but it was added that "there is an indefinite delay and no calls are being accepted."

Senate Votes 50 Million to War Refugees

CHAPTER 11

The New Bug

FIGHT TUBERCULOSIS with MODERN WEAPONS

Christ-
mas Seals
help fight
Tuberculosis

THE NURSE'S AIDE put down her bucket and took a stack of washcloths out from under her flabby arm. She was a former patient who insisted we call her Miss Wanda. She looked over at the bed next to mine. "I see we got a new bug. What's her name?"

"Sarah Morgan," Pearl answered, playing the welcome hostess for our room.

Sarah was in the bed closest to me, the one where the other girl had died. I wouldn't tell Sarah about Marianne, especially because this new girl looked so small and thin, more sickly even than the rest of us. But what would I tell her? *Here's Dena. She knows too much and will scare the dickens out of you. Then there's Pearl. She thinks she's a queen and expects everyone to pay attention to her. I'm Evvy—the one with no friends and a healthy twin brother back home. And finally Beverly, with her pretty blond braids. She's so kind and perfect, you feel like you're living with a Sunday-school teacher.*

Miss Wanda slopped a watery washcloth across Sarah's face. The new girl squinched her eyes shut, then started to cough. A chattering, garbled sound came up from her chest as if she'd rumbled marbles loose in her lungs.

Miss Wanda took a big step back. "Whoa! You'd better take it easy, Sarah. Too much coughin' can bring on the coffin! That's what happened to Marianne."

"Cut it out," I barked.

Sarah's eyes fluttered open, seeming to find their focus only when they landed on me. Did the new girl want me to help or just leave her alone? Her dark eyes closed again without giving me a hint.

"Well, hear the old-timer Evelyn Hoffmeister speak." Miss Wanda strolled around to pick up the wet washcloths. "Maybe Sarah has some news about the war to share. You may not care about the Nazis, Evelyn *Hoffmeister*, but the rest of us might."

Miss Wanda wasn't the first person to make me feel bad because of my German name. Some kids had taunted us on the playground. Abe told me, "They're idiots, Ev. Don't let 'em get to you." I just hadn't figured grown-ups could be idiots too.

Miss Wanda kept talking. "Who's to say one of your uncles isn't driving his U-boat up the Mississippi River right now to come get you!"

"Put a sock in it!" Dena called from across the room. "No submarines are coming up the Mississippi River. They stay in the ocean."

Miss Wanda grabbed a folded newspaper from the large pocket on her apron and flashed it just long enough so we could all see the words "Nazi" and "Paris" in the headline. "They're parading through Paris, attacking England. They've already taken Holland and Belgium. We're next—just you wait!"

My stomach tightened. If Abe were here, he'd know if what Miss Wanda said was true or not. He'd stuck a map of Europe up on his bedroom wall, marking with pushpins each country Hitler had taken. Was she right? Would America soon join the fight?

Miss Wanda gathered her supplies, kicked aside the doorstop, then called over her shoulder, "Don't come screaming to me when a Nazi stares in the window some night, ready to get you!"

I threw off my covers, angry and frustrated. Miss Wanda acted like the Nazis were a whole new kind of germ about to swarm this place and attack us all. Wasn't our fight against TB battle enough?

CHAPTER 12

Blue Nothing

TWO DAYS AFTER the new girl, Sarah, arrived, I got my first privilege. I would be allowed to sit up— or rather, get propped up on pillows—and receive mail!

"Don't get too excited, Evvy," Dena said when the meal trays were finally taken away. "Letters are never as good as you want 'em to be."

"Oh, yes they are," Pearl insisted, wagging her hairbrush at Dena. "You're just jealous. My best friend, Muriel, writes me the longest, best letters just full of news."

"Yeah, I know what her letters are full of . . ."

Pearl turned to look at me as if that could make Dena disappear and kept talking. "Plus, Evvy, you can get magazines like *Photoplay*—oh, and the *Loon Lake Booster* too." Pearl returned to her mirror and finished smoothing her hair into soft curls.

"Yeah, there's something to really cheer you up," Dena said. "A newsletter written by a bunch of lungers. What could bring a smile to your sick face faster than some Pollyannas telling you their plucky little stories?"

"Well, I like the *Booster*," Pearl said. "It certainly does boost my spirits!"

Pearl sounded like one of those too-cheerful voices on the radio pushing a new and improved product.

"I promise to take a look at it," I said, hoping to end all talk of the *Booster*. "I really just hope to hear from my brother."

"What's his name?" Beverly asked with polite interest.

"Abe—well, really Abraham—but no one ever calls him that, except maybe my mother sometimes."

"You mean like Honest Abe?" Dena said, half chuckling.

"Nope, not Abraham Lincoln," I said. "He was named after my mother's great-grandfather who played the cornet at President James Buchanan's inauguration."

"Abraham's a Hebrew name from the Old Testament," Sarah said without opening her eyes.

This was the first time since her arrival she'd said anything in the way of conversation. I'd decided having Sarah in the bed next to me was about as exciting as having another white wall added to our room. Now it seemed like the wall knew a thing or two about the Bible.

"Is your brother older than you, Evvy?" Beverly asked.

"Yeah, but just by a couple of minutes. We're twins." I'd never told them before about having a twin brother—which was usually the first fact most people knew about me.

"Identical?" Pearl said, perking up with delight.

"No. We can't be, since he's a boy and I'm a girl," I explained for probably the millionth time in my life. "We're fraternal twins."

"Oh," said Pearl, sounding disappointed. I could tell she was already dressing us in adorable matching outfits in her mind's eye. "So do you two even look alike?"

Sarah opened her eyes and turned her face in my direction.

"People say we do, but I don't think so. Abe's got blondish hair, mine's browner. I've got green eyes, his are more hazel. He's really tall for his age, I'm not."

I've got TB, he doesn't. He gets along with Mother, I don't. He's great in music and math, I'm hopeless in both.

Dena pointed her finger at me, then mumbled "Old Eagle Eye" just an instant before Nurse Marshall stepped into the room. She delivered the mail to the other girls first. More letters for Beverly, a new *Photoplay* for Pearl, nothing for Dena. Pearl held up her magazine and posed her face alongside, hoping I'd notice how she resembled the actress on the cover. She did, but I didn't need to encourage her more.

Finally Nurse Marshall stopped at my bed and tucked two pillows behind my back. I felt a little woozy sitting up, like my brain had rolled down to visit my toes. I looked out with new eyes at the room around me. It was both bigger and emptier than I'd imagined. The windows seemed to pop into three dimensions, as if they'd only been flat paintings before. I could also see more of the trees and two different buildings far off.

Then Nurse Marshall handed me my mail. I let my fingers slide back and forth across the paper envelopes. My hands seemed hungry to feel something other than bedsheets. I counted the letters.

Only six. Somehow I had thought there would be more.

I felt Sarah's eyes watching me and gave a quick smile in her direction, not wanting to seem like a letter hog. She didn't smile back but looked down at my mail as if to remind me I still needed to read my letters. I felt suddenly shy at having an audience but eager all the same to read the news from home.

Just one letter was from Abe. I put it aside for last.

I opened the three from Mother. Each letter began the same way:

Dearest Evelyn, I hope this letter finds you in improving health.

Then she told me the same kind of polite news she wrote to her mother in St. Louis once a week. I found myself sitting up straighter—as if Mother had reminded me about good posture—when she described the minister's visit for tea or her meeting with the dean of music from St. Olaf College.

Fortunately, Father ended each letter with some silly comment about our garden:

You are the sprout in my Brussels, the snap in my beans, the kernels in my corn. Peas get well soon.

Next I read a letter from each of my grandmothers. Grandmother Brimley—Mother's mother—lived in St. Louis, so I hardly ever saw her. She wrote such a somber, formal letter that I almost wondered if I'd died already. She never called my disease by its name; instead she referred to it as "my struggle." I could already feel myself getting crabby about having to write her back.

My father's mother, Grandma Hoffmeister, wrote a totally different letter. For one thing, I knew this grandmother. She lived in Kenyon, a little town close to Northfield, and often came to visit, even more after my grandfather passed away. She spoke with a strong German accent—and seemed to write with one as well. Her bold, no-nonsense handwriting charged across the page at me so strongly that I held the letter out at a distance to read it.

She told me that the cost of meat was going up— all the fault of the war in Europe—and that she had baked three cakes last week for the church and was sorry I wasn't there to help scrape and lick the left-over batter from the bowl.

She didn't make any attempt to sound cheerful.

> You are giving gray hairs
> on zee heads of your parents.
> Get well and get home!

I could imagine her wagging her finger at me—
sort of Grandma's way of showing her love. At some
point I would write her about how much I missed
her cakes, knowing that when I did get well, she'd
bake a triple-layer chocolate cake with icing just
for me.

I saved Abe's letter for last, certain it would be
the best. I pulled it slowly out of the envelope. It was
written on a sheet of paper colored with dark layers
of blue crayon. The words, scratched out of the wax,
were blurry but still readable. Soon my fingers, too,
were smeared with blue.

Dear Evvy,
I wish I could come see you, but
Mother says that we can't yet and I
have to write you instead. Oh, buzzards!
You know how I hate to write. Does
this count as a letter? It should,
because it's a misstery too.

Love,
Abe

I read and reread Abe's letter. I flipped it over
and examined both sides. I looked back at the envelope. Even the stamp he'd chosen was blue!

I knew he didn't like writing, but was this it?

And what did he mean by a mystery? Didn't he even know how to spell that word? Maybe not, since he was always lousy at spelling. But still, there was no mystery, except maybe why he wrote so little. I'd been counting on him to tell me what was really going on at home. He could have at least told me he was miserable and missed me. Or about his stupid trumpet. Or about the neighbor's cat, who was supposed to have kittens right when I left. Something! He could have thought of something to tell me.

Dena was right. Letters do disappoint. I'd waited all this time for nothing: a rotten blue, blurry nothing from Abe.

CHAPTER 13

Blue Something

"YOUR BROTHER is clever," a voice whispered after the lights were out.

Who's talking? Not Dena or Beverly. Certainly not Pearl. It was Sarah, and as my eyes adjusted to the wash of moonlight coming in through the window, I could see her looking at me, her wavy dark hair framing her face.

But why is she talking? And about Abe?

"I saw the letter he wrote you—earlier today, I mean." Her dark eyes demanded my attention, as if she had important business. "He colored it blue!"

"Yeah, it was blue," I said, irritated that my smudged fingers seemed to have gotten more out of the letter than I had.

"He did that for a reason, Evvy."

Hearing someone so close whisper my name felt both strange and exciting, as if we were in a secret hideout instead of a sickroom. "A reason?"

"I like solving puzzles. I kept wondering why he'd take the time to color a piece of paper with blue crayons." Sarah took shallow, fast breaths, as if to keep up with the rush of her thoughts. "Just blue. And to scratch out the words like that. Then it hit me. He's feeling blue, Evvy. He misses you. He just colored it instead of saying it!"

Could that be true? Abe did hate writing, especially letters. Coloring with a blue crayon sounded just like some scheme he'd come up with to dodge writing lots of words.

"Okay," I said, sorting it through aloud. "He's blue and he misses me. . . . And that's why he said the letter was a *miss*tery!"

Sarah laughed—a warbly, playful giggle that

seemed to leap across the space between our beds and make me laugh too.

"Shhh," someone cautioned us from across the room.

I waited a moment, not about to let anyone end this conversation, then whispered, "That's pretty smart of you, Sarah. How old are you?"

"Just turned fourteen. You?"

"Thirteen still."

"I'm no Sherlock Holmes, Evvy—only jealous because I can't get mail."

I spoke in an even softer whisper. "Beverly has a whole stack, and Pearl gets loads of letters from her friend Muriel."

Sarah whispered back to me, "Probably none as clever as Abe's."

I didn't want to be in Abe's shadow right now, or admit how unclever I'd thought he was before. "You'll get letters from your brothers and sisters before long."

Sarah's hair swished on the pillow. "Can't—I'm an only child."

"Well, I could loan you Abe!" I suggested, watching her face in the milky light. "But be warned, he practices his trumpet all the time. He wants to be the next Louis Armstrong."

Sarah smiled as she considered my offer, then asked, "Do you play something?"

"Not anymore. I stunk so bad at the clarinet that Abe renamed me Evvy Badman."

Sarah thought for a second, then laughed. "I get it. You're no Benny Goodman."

I laughed too, glad something amusing had come out of all the squeaks and squawks I'd made on the clarinet. "How about you, Sarah? Do you play anything?"

"I played the violin for a little while—till my teacher said I'd never perform at Carnegie Hall. That's when my parents decided the lessons cost too much."

I was glad to know I wasn't the only daughter who'd disappointed her parents for lacking musical talent.

Sarah shifted in her bed and cleared her throat into a tissue.

"You'll get letters from friends," I told her, not wanting to admit I didn't expect to hear from any girls I knew unless their parents made them write me.

"I don't really have any friends. I skipped two grades at school," she said, though not in a bragging way. "Kids call me a know-it-all behind my back."

"Yeah, well, I wouldn't mind being smart. I still don't know all my state capitals, and I don't get why you use parentheses in algebra. Don't they belong in language class?"

Sarah thought I was trying to be funny and laughed. I didn't mind, since I was used to playing second fiddle to Abe. Plus, I liked Sarah paying attention to me—just me.

"I guess—" A quick, skittery blast of coughs stopped her from saying more.

"Cut the chatter!" This time I recognized Dena's voice. "Ya don't wanna make Nurse Gunderson mad."

Dena was right, but I still gave Sarah my I-hate-the-rules-here look. Sarah pulled the sheet up to her chin, and we both settled down to sleep.

Now the quiet didn't seem so empty. I'd just had a conversation! A real conversation—a friendly one! Thoughts flip-flopped around inside my head. From Sarah to Abe, to my letters, back to Sarah, then finally on to something else—Dena.

Why had Dena warned us? She never seemed to care before what happened in our room. Was she really worried about upsetting Nurse Gunderson, or just jealous about Sarah being friendly to me? I'd never understand Dena, and I sure wasn't going to let her ruin my chances of getting to know Sarah.

CHAPTER 14

The Giant

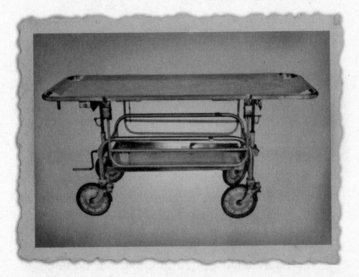

I WOKE UP from my morning rest to Nurse Marshall swooping about our room, diving in close to check on us, then flying off to look down the corridor.

Had something happened?

I heard the usual coughs and wheezes. Everyone looked okay to me.

Then, from somewhere far down the hall, I

heard a faint thump. Then another and another, each sounding louder and closer—like a giant stomping toward our room.

Thump! Thump! *Thump!*

All eyes were now open, all of us listening.

Between the thumps I heard the jangle of wheels rattling—as if the giant pulled a wagon behind him.

Louder and closer.

Louder! Closer!

Then Nurse Marshall pushed our heavy door shut. *Thump!*

The giant's wagon rumbled down the hall, past our room.

No one coughed or moved or even breathed.

Then the giant and his noise were gone.

As if a switch had been flipped, doors that had thumped closed now reopened, coughs sputtered back up, Nurse Marshall returned to her tasks—the sanatorium resumed its monotonous routine.

What was that? I wanted to know, but no one said anything.

I looked at Sarah. Her face looked tight and pale. She closed her eyes, turned her head away from me, and seemed to breathe in short, sniffly bursts.

Then Dena, on her way to see Dr. Tollerud for her pneumo, ducked her head in my direction and muttered, "A lunger got carted home this morning."

I thought for a moment, sorry I was the one who had to explain this to Sarah. I almost wished I could bury the sad truth under layers of Grandmother Brimley's formal talk. But I couldn't. The words stirred up inside me. "Sarah, what Dena said about a patient going home—"

"Don't!" Sarah cried, pressing her hands against her ears. "Don't say anything, Evvy! I know what happened."

"But I—"

Nurse Marshall stormed into the room and looked from Sarah to me. "Evil-in, what did you say to her?"

"N-nothing," I stammered, but it felt like I was holding a bloody dagger in my hand. Why was Sarah so angry at me? What had I done?

Nurse Marshall bent over Sarah. I waited to hear the nurse's order for Sarah to stop crying. None came.

I turned my back to them both and felt my own pillow grow damp with tears.

CHAPTER 15

Moving Pictures

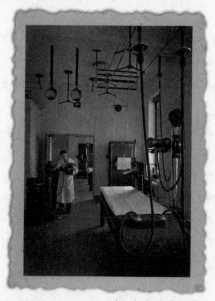

"YOU AND BEVERLY are scheduled for fluoroscopy in ten minutes," Nurse Marshall said, her eagle eye aimed directly at me. I didn't know what fluoroscopy was but hoped it didn't hurt. "Evil-in, you will go in a wheelchair. Beverly, I trust you are capable of pushing her."

For some reason, this news irritated Pearl. She glanced at Beverly, then shoved back her tray table and slid down under her blankets.

I'd taken to watching Pearl, who added a touch of drama to everything she did—from brushing her hair with long, sweeping gestures to pointing her toes when she slipped her legs out from under the covers. I wondered if she did all this knowing I was paying attention. But now, under her blankets, she was as quiet and still as Sarah, who seemed uncomfortable even at the sight of me now. The white wall had returned.

Beverly slid out of bed while Nurse Marshall helped me sit up and move to the wheelchair. The room swirled around in my head, then circled back into place, my twitchy hands holding tight to the armrests. I felt a brush of braids against my shoulders and looked to see Beverly behind the chair. Then we were off.

The hallways were noisy and busy. My pulse jumped to keep up with the flurry of activity. Beverly leaned over and said, "It's a moving picture of your lungs, sort of an X-ray in motion."

I nodded and pretended to understand but was distracted by a rushing, pounding sound—like faucets being turned on and off full force inside my ears. Was that my own heart beating so loudly? Is that why I needed the flurry, the floro, the fluro—whatever we were off to get?

Beverly soon stopped us outside a tall door. Maybe she could hear my heart pounding, because she put her hands atop my shoulders and patted me gently, rhythmically. For a moment I thought she was Mother, who was always tapping out musical beats to instruct her students. I closed my eyes and let the rhythm soothe me, then realized what Beverly had been trying to tell me about the procedure.

And she was right. The fluoroscopy was just a different sort of X-ray. It didn't hurt, though I struggled to keep up with the doctor's commands to move my arm this way or to tilt my head that way, and I felt exhausted by the time it was over.

I was done first, then had to wait with Beverly for her turn. She rested on a bench beside me, calm and quiet, so I was surprised when she tipped her head and said, "She was scared, Evvy. That's all. Don't be angry with her."

I tugged at a loose thread on my robe. "You mean Sarah?"

"Mmm."

"I'm not angry at her, Beverly." But even I could hear the lie in my voice. "Anyway, it doesn't matter what I feel. She doesn't like me."

I twisted the snapped thread between my fingers

and waited for Beverly to tell me I was wrong, to make me feel better. Instead she asked, "Do you think I like Pearl and Dena, Evvy?"

I laughed. "How could you? They're both stinkers—I mean, they fight like cats and dogs all the time."

Beverly leaned her head forward, then said with a hint of amusement, "They do, don't they."

I took her response as encouragement to say more. "You're always trying to make them get along, and they never do—and they probably never will!"

"True again, Evvy."

I kept going, glad to say aloud what I'd been thinking since I'd arrived three months ago. "And you just pretend to smile, as if that will make things all better."

I regretted my words as soon as I said them. I hadn't meant to criticize Beverly. Her smiles—real or fake—were better than Pearl and Dena's squabbles any day.

Beverly shook her head, the two braids swooshing across her robe. "I'm not pretending, Evvy. We all have our own ways to get by here. Dena and Pearl too."

"You mean, you like them?"

Beverly nodded, then smiled—this time right at me. "I understand them, Evvy."

The door to the office opened and the doctor signaled Beverly to come inside for her fluoroscopy. As she stood up, she said, "Try understanding Sarah a little. She may not be as brave as you, but you're going to need each other—we all do."

Me? Brave? Why would anyone think that?

But that night, when the others were asleep, I leaned over and whispered in Sarah's direction, "I cried when I found out too. I bet everybody does."

A thin voice answered. "But does everybody think they're going to be the one who'll die next?"

A cold shiver ran through me. "Probably—any one of us could. But I gotta see Abe again, and you gotta"—I paused, not sure what to say—"and you gotta be a know-it-all scientist or nurse or doctor and make things better for people."

Sarah seemed to sigh and laugh at once. "Could I maybe see Abe sometime too?"

"As long as you never tell him he helped us. He likes to blow his own horn enough already!"

August 3, 1940

Dear Family,

    I haven't seen any loons or the lake yet, but that's because I've been following the doctor's orders and resting in bed. I like getting your letters. I can't write a lot now. I hope you're all well. I miss you very much.

                      Love,
                      Evvy

PS—Abe, I RED your letter.

PPS—Father, you are the pep in my pepper.

CHAPTER 16

Out of Breath

"TIME'S UP," Nurse Marshall instructed before I could think of a PS just for Mother to end my letter.

I folded the paper and placed it in the addressed envelope, lifting it to my lips to seal it shut.

"What are you doing, Evil-in!" Nurse Marshall bellowed. "Have you no sense? Do you want millions of germs to be mailed to your family? *Never, ever* lick an envelope at Loon Lake."

My throat tightened as Nurse Marshall snatched the letter out of the envelope, addressed a new one, then pressed the flap against a drop of water poured onto the cleaned bedside table. Why hadn't I noticed the other girls doing that before?

Little coughs started to hatch one after the next from my mouth. I gulped some milk, but between that going down one way and the air coming up the other, a volcanic coughing fit erupted. I shoved a handful of tissues to my lips, trying to hold the coughs back.

Even with Nurse Marshall glaring down at me, I couldn't stop. My lungs kept playing tug-of-war with the walls of my chest.

Then something like glue splattered yellow and pink across the tissue in my hand.

"You must breathe, Evil-in," Nurse Marshall coached, as if I didn't know that already.

But the coughing got worse. Stars swirled in front of my eyes. I swung my hands up and grabbed at Nurse Marshall. I wanted to scream but had no voice to form the words.

"Do something!" Dena yelled at Nurse Marshall. "She's turning blue. Can't ya do something?"

Nurse Marshall pushed me flat against the bed and tilted my head back, then jimmied my mouth open and reached down inside my throat with her curled fingers.

My body twisted, my legs spinning knots into the sheet.

Nurse Marshall bobbed forward, then pulled her

glistening hand out of my mouth. A frothy, gurgling gasp seemed to trail behind her slippery fingers.

"Breathe, Evvy. Breathe, breathe," Sarah said. The others joined the chant.

I found one breath. Then another.

Dr. Keith appeared at Nurse Marshall's side. He sat me upright in bed and smacked his palm between my shoulder blades as I sucked in more and more air.

He then ordered Nurse Marshall to go clean herself up immediately. She hesitated, but he insisted. "You know yourself that the patient aspirated on some of her own secretions. This was not hemoptysis. Now my concern is for your safety, Nurse Marshall. We cannot risk losing another nurse. I will stay until the patient is resting."

He turned back to me, checking my eyes with a small flashlight.

As soon as both Nurse Marshall and Dr. Keith had left, Dena translated Dr. Keith's diagnosis into language the rest of us could understand. "Evvy choked, that's all. She didn't throw a ruby. No blood. Just gunk going down the wrong pipe. Could have happened to anybody. Evvy's okay for now. It wasn't the big one."

August 13, 1940

Dearest Evelyn,

   I hope your health continues to improve, despite the recent incident. On Monday, Father spoke to Dr. Keith, who reassured us that you are much better now and making steady progress.

   Your father's garden is flourishing, which means we have already exhausted all of Grandma Hoffmeister's cabbage recipes. Fortunately for your father, Abe has stepped in to help while you are at Loon Lake.

   Since I'm not giving voice lessons at present, my time now is occupied with activities at church and at home. I volunteered to sort through boxes of choral music left untouched for years in the church basement. Much of it deserves to remain there, but I have found noteworthy pieces as well, which I hope the choir will choose to perform at some future date. I have even found some trumpet music to challenge Abe and practice with him to polish my own skills as a piano accompanist.

   As always,
   Your Loving Mother

PS—A note from your cabbage-crazy father:

Dr. Keith says you're a real pip, Puddlejump. Good to hear. And don't believe a word your mother says about your brother being a help in the garden. He's got such a black thumb that I bet even the corn is shocked! You best get well soon and hurry home to help me. Your mother, too. If she's not moping, she's mopping. A fellow can't step foot in this house without getting a lecture on wiping his feet.

Love you, Evvy. You always tickle my potaTOES! Father

PPS—Abe promises to write you another letter soon. Hmm . . . We can hope!

CHAPTER 17

Flying Away

PLEASE

"WHAT A MUGGY August night," Nurse Gunderson said as she started around to take our temperatures. "You must all be thirsty."

"Not for more prune juice," Dena grumbled.

Nurse Gunderson tipped her head and gave Dena a sly look. "My girls certainly have earned a break from prune juice! When I finish my work, I have a little surprise."

A surprise! A good surprise at Loon Lake! Sarah and I gave each other puzzled, happy looks as Nurse Gunderson moved from bed to bed in slow motion—or at least that's how it felt.

At last done with our temperatures, she reached over and, like a magician, lifted a towel from atop the cart. "Ta-da!"

There in front of us rested six bottles of cola. I had not seen that familiar pale green bottle since I'd arrived at Loon Lake. "Wow!"

"I thought a little treat would do us all some good," Nurse Gunderson said, popping off the caps to open the bottles, the soda bubbles fizzling upward like little fireworks. "I wish I could get you a radio, but Dr. Tollerud—well, it's just not allowed."

She stuck a straw into each bottle, then handed the drinks around. I pulled the straw to my lips and took my first sip. The bubbles tickled and teased the whole way down, the satisfying and familiar flavor almost making up for so much prune juice, too much milk, and—the worst—buttermilk. Almost.

Nurse Gunderson took a bottle for herself and sat down in a chair by the window, untying her mask to enjoy the August night air with us. "Let me tell you about the stars I see out your window tonight. Of course, there's the Big Dipper. But that looks too much like a sputum cup for me."

We laughed, and she gave us a playful frown to remind us to keep quiet.

"Oh, I can spot Pegasus over there," she went on, pointing up to the sky. "Wouldn't it be wonderful to fly away on a winged horse like Pegasus?"

I'd never heard a grown-up talk about something as imaginary as flying on a winged horse before.

"You know," she said, "I have a real horse named Willow back home. I guess it's not fair for me to call her my horse anymore, since my sisters and brothers take care of her now—like I take care of all of you. But I do wish I could see Willow sometime soon. Maybe Pegasus up there could loan me some wings."

Our eyes followed hers upward, out the window, then to our own imagined heavens, where we could hold on to Pegasus and ride across the sky—all airborne, all safe, all well, all together.

Then Beverly coughed, and Nurse Gunderson drifted back down from the stars—with us trailing behind her—and settled into our room again.

I'd gotten so used to seeing the nurses wearing their little white masks that I'd almost forgotten how comforting a smile could be.

She placed her empty bottle on the windowsill, then rested her head against the wall and closed her eyes. The warm night air made us all sleepy.

Sarah and I exchanged lazy smiles, and I put my bottle down and closed my eyes too.

I might have slept straight till morning had I not heard faint whispering from across the room.

"Should I wake Nurse Gunderson?" Pearl asked Dena.

"Nah, let her rest," Dena answered. "She's tired."

"I just don't want her to get in trouble," Pearl said.

Dena nodded, and they both got out of bed—Beverly too.

Pearl collected the empty cola bottles and hid them back under the towel on the cart. Beverly crumpled the paper straws in a ball and tucked them beneath a tissue in the paper bag alongside her bed. Dena scooped up the bottle caps, ready to throw them away too, but instead took an envelope, dropped the six caps inside, and tucked the bumpy envelope into her drawer.

Then a sweet peace settled over our room. The next time I woke up, Nurse Gunderson and the cart were both gone.

LEARN AND LIVE WITH

The Loon Lake Booster

NEWS YOU CAN USE TO GIVE YOU A BOOST

September 1940   Volume 126

The Poetry Corner

HOPE IN HAND
by
W. D. Sibley

One day I held
    A little seed
And found in it
    The hope I need.
How could I cry
    Or moan my plight?
Or hide my soul
    In darkest night?
When in my hand
    I held the key
To greet each day
    More joyfully.
For if a seed
    In time could be
A tall, majestic,
    Healthy tree
Then I could also
    Wish to stand,
Free of illness,
    Hope in hand.

Loon Lake Patient of the Month
A Blue Ribbon Winner!

BETTY JORGENSON has always been a winner. Just ask those who know her best. Ward mate Darlene Krislow says, "Betty's smile brightens our ward every day." Nurse Martha Roseblum agrees. "Her cheerful disposition brings delight to all. And her healthy attitude is helping her body heal."

Imagine Betty's thrill when her own needlepoint was entered and won a blue ribbon at the county fair. Betty's stitchery pays special tribute to life at Loon Lake Sanatorium. Her design shows a beautiful loon on the lake at sunrise. Below she stitched the touching words: "The Loon Calls Forth a Cure."

Congratulations, Betty Jorgenson, our Loon Lake Patient of the Month—and a real winner!

The Loon Lake Pledge

I promise I will let my
body heal and rest.
I pledge to greet each
day with a smile.
My cure begins
with me.

Upcoming Concert

A special evening
of violin music to
inspire us all will
be held in the
courtyard, Sunday
evening at 7:00 P.M.

LUCKY LOON REMINDS YOU . . .

"Every cough strains your lungs and hinders your healing. So give your lungs a rest, and soon you'll be back in the swim of things!"

Remember:
Lucky loon loves healthy lungs!

A Boost

"I HOPE THE *BOOSTER* will print my poem when I finish it," said Pearl. "Nurse Gunderson already thinks my title, 'Our Spirits, Too, Will Soar,' is perfect!"

"Perfectly sore," Dena jabbed.

Sarah lifted her head. "I think Evvy should write a poem. She has a way with words."

I felt my ears tingle. I'd told Sarah how I liked to learn new words, but that didn't mean I could write poems or stories. Still, it was nice Sarah thought I could.

"Evvy may know a few words to solve crossword puzzles," Pearl said, wagging her copy of the *Loon Lake Booster*, "but that's not the same as having the ability to create poetry! Writing poetry demands maturity of body and spirit."

Sarah rolled her eyes in my direction, ready to knock the crown off Pearl's queenly head. Pearl had become even more difficult ever since she'd gotten permission for a day visit with her older brother, Edmund, two months from now in November. I gave Sarah one of my here-we-go-again looks, secretly glad to have something else to share with her.

Pearl reached for a pen and notepad from her bedside table. "I think I'll use a true love story as inspiration for my poem!"

"Quit blowing on and on about *Gone with the Wind*, will ya!" Dena said.

"I'm talking about a *true* love story, Dena. One right from the halls of Loon Lake. Between our own Nurse Gunderson and Dr. Keith!"

Dena glared at Pearl out of the corner of her eye. "You're full of hooey."

"I am not!" Pearl whined. "I heard it from one of the older girls yesterday. Dr. Keith is head over heels in love with our Nurse Gunderson. It's a secret because Dr. Tollerud wouldn't approve. I just thought you were all too juvenile to know such things. I mean, most of you haven't even started your monthlies yet . . ."

Pearl paused just long enough so we could all

appreciate that she got a period while the rest of us didn't. I pulled the sheet up to my shoulders, embarrassed by my own lack of progress in the turning-into-a-woman department.

Dena couldn't keep quiet. "I count living with you as my monthly curse!"

"If it's true," said Beverly, "then I'm happy for her. They make a lovely couple."

"Oh yes, it is true," Pearl said, just as the bell rang to start the Cure Hour.

Beverly was right: they would make a lovely couple. But somehow other thoughts kept creeping into my mind.

All my life, I'd heard people call my own parents "a lovely couple." I always figured it meant my mother was pretty and my father was handsome. But now I thought about the word *couple*. Being part of a couple was different from being part of a family.

Sometimes I wished Father would see how difficult Mother could be, how she wasn't always lovely. But he didn't. When my father walked in the door after work, he kissed me on the head and said, "Evening, Puddlejump." But he wasn't really home until his eyes fell on my mother, and she smiled and said his name so it sounded like music. Why did they have to be a couple first, before we could be a family?

And now I worried Nurse Gunderson might leave us to be part of a couple too.

I thought about what Abe once said after we caught our parents kissing: "Grown-ups make about as much sense as a goat wearing glasses."

LOON LAKE SANATORIUM
WEIGHT CHART

Patient Number: **22781**
Patient Name: Evelyn Hoffmeister
DOB: 4-9-1927
Admitted: 5-2-1940

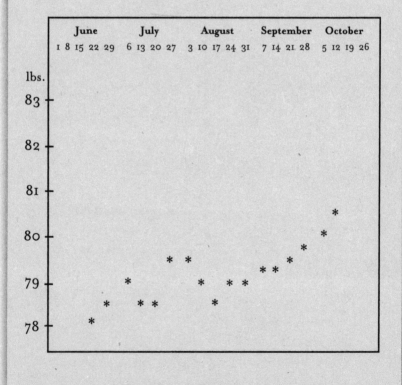

CHAPTER 19

Numbers

"DO YOU EVER see numbers, Evvy?" Sarah asked as we sat side by side in wheelchairs, waiting our turn to get weighed. We were looking out the window at the oak trees, their October leaves turning from red to brown.

I could feel my ears start to redden. "I hoped I wasn't that obvious."

"Obvious about what, Evvy?" Sarah asked, tilting her head. Her cheeks were flushed, but her lips looked pale.

"You know, peeking at my weight when anyone writes it down."

"Oh, we all do that," she said. "No, I mean when you have a fever. Do you ever see numbers?"

"Nope. Not numbers. I see waves and lots of water."

"Hmm, waves," Sarah said. She swayed slightly, as if being washed over by one. "I see numbers, Evvy. Streams of numbers. When the fever begins, they come faster and faster, millions and millions of numbers, and they all race through me like—"

"Like electricity?"

"That's it!" she said. "Exactly!"

Even with a fever, Sarah watched and reacted to things I said—like she was reading me, not just skimming along.

A clattering, jingling noise from out in the hallway quieted us both. Miss Wanda opened the door, and my stomach tightened. "Oh look, it's my two sweet apples," she said, dragging in the scales and wedging them between us. She reached as if to give my cheek a pinch. "Such sweet apples, but still so rotten at the core."

Was that true? Were we rotting away inside?

I wished Dena were here to snap back at Miss Wanda. But Dena, Pearl, and Beverly, who were allowed to be up attending classes again, had gone down the hall to use the more reliable scales. Sarah and I were still on room restriction, so the scales came to us—clanking and complaining the whole way and, sadly, bringing Miss Wanda along. She signaled for an orderly to come weigh us, then left, saying, "Bye-bye, little apples."

All TB patients hated getting weighed. If you didn't gain weight, you felt like the germs were jumping up and down inside your lungs, knowing they were winning.

If you did gain weight, you got privileges. Three additional pounds for me meant I got to start feeding myself and reading for an hour a day. A few more today and I might get to use the bathroom toilet instead of a bedpan. These scales measured our success—and our failure.

Sarah sucked in air—as if that could add more weight—and was lifted onto the scale. I felt my eyes stealing a quick look. Sarah was losing, not gaining. My news was better: I'd gained a pound. Not enough to earn my next privilege, but good all the same.

Still, I hated feeling like this was a competition. "You must be doing better, Sarah, or else Dr. Keith wouldn't let you get mail."

She coughed, then wiped her mouth on a tissue. "Maybe he knows that getting letters from my parents isn't much of a privilege."

I shot Sarah a smile. We'd joked before about how dull letters from our parents could be. But she didn't smile back. Instead she hunched forward, small and too quiet.

I tried to ignore the angry chatter of the scales as they left our room.

But I couldn't ignore Sarah. I couldn't be sure I was getting better, but I was pretty sure Sarah was getting worse.

D.O.

DISCHARGE ORDER

LOON LAKE SANATORIUM

Dr. F. H. Tollerud, Medical Director

OFFICIAL DOCUMENT

The attached document, once completed and signed by the Attending Physician and the Medical Director, certifies that the patient named herein has been officially discharged from Loon Lake Sanatorium and is no longer the responsibility of said Institution or Staff.

Summary of Hospitalization Records Must Be Obtained Separately by Contacting the Medical Director's Office

CHAPTER 20

Discharged

PEARL STARTED jabbering as soon as Nurse Marshall stepped out of the room. Not to me or to Sarah but back and forth to Beverly and Dena.

"It probably doesn't have anything to do with us," I heard Dena tell Pearl.

"But I saw it, Dena. In her hands. I just know it has to be mine!" Pearl's cheeks flushed with anticipation.

Beverly sat up in bed. "I say we all settle down. No need to get excited yet." But I could tell Beverly was stirred up too.

"Is there news?" Sarah asked in her raspy, waking-up voice.

Dena grumbled. "Who knows? Pearl thinks she saw a discharge order on Nurse Marshall's morning clipboard."

"What does that mean?" I asked.

"One of us might be sprung out of this joint," Dena answered. "Discharged."

Sarah and I exchanged glances. I knew that even with my recent progress it couldn't be me, and Sarah—well, not Sarah either. That left Pearl, Beverly, and Dena—if Pearl really had seen the form.

"Well, of course, it's my turn," Pearl announced. "I follow the rules, I have a positive attitude, and I even pinned my hair up last night. I must have a sixth sense about such things." Pearl raced to take out the bobby pins. "I guess I'll be surprising my brother instead of him surprising me!"

"If TB played fair and we took turns," Dena told her, "I'd have been out of here a long time ago. Four years I've been waiting."

Four years! Could I last that long? Could Sarah?

Pearl tipped her head forward to loosen more curls at the nape of her neck. "Really, Dena, it's not like this is some dance marathon, and the winner is the person who lasts the longest."

"You wanna bet?" Dena snorted.

Pearl brushed out her hair, as if that could rid the

room of snarls and doubts at once. "Why, I could be home in time for October Homecoming!" she said with increasing excitement. "Of course, I'd need new clothes to wear. A dress—no, a suit would be better. Something smart. A wool plaid maybe. And new shoes. Muriel will know just the thing—"

"Quit adding an imaginary wardrobe to your imaginary discharge form," Dena said.

Pearl fluffed her curls with the palm of her hand. "I didn't imagine that discharge order. You'll see— and soon. Nurse Marshall will be back in a few minutes."

We all got quiet, as if Nurse Marshall were standing at our beds already.

We waited with ferocious attention to every footstep in the corridor, to every conversation overheard outside the door, to every move made by a staff member in our room. None of us asked Nurse Marshall about the discharge, as if that might put a jinx on things. We couldn't ask Nurse Gunderson either. She hadn't been to our room in weeks, though it felt like months, since we all missed her. Dena figured they'd rotated her to another ward, or maybe let her take a vacation before the first snow arrived.

By the time lights were out for the night, Pearl

was in tears. Everyone but Dena tried to console her, but even Dena was worn out and stopped challenging Pearl about the discharge form. I felt like we'd all been invited to a special party that got canceled at the last minute.

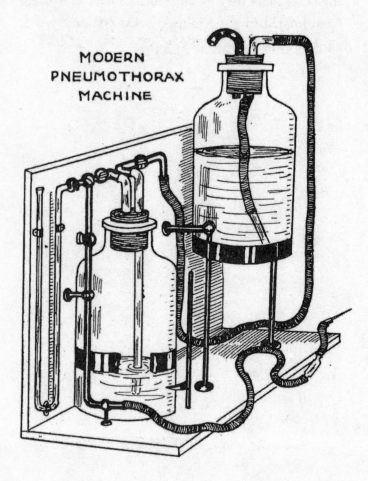

MODERN
PNEUMOTHORAX
MACHINE

CHAPTER 21

Looking Back

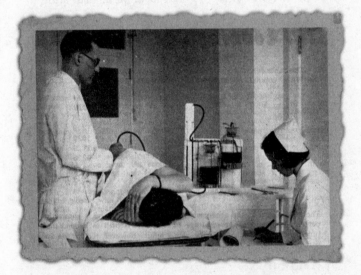

THE NEXT MORNING, when I woke up, I found that I'd tugged all the sheets and blankets loose from my bed. They draped to the floor like sails untied from their rigging.

Why hadn't Nurse Marshall come in to fix my bedding? And where was everybody? The other beds were unmade—and empty. Could they all have been discharged?

Father liked to say, "If you run around like a chicken with its head cut off, you'll end up in hot soup!" Right now the soup was feeling plenty warm. *Think logically, Evvy. Like Sarah would. Dena, Pearl, and Beverly must be off at class. Sarah must be getting a fluoroscope. See? All perfectly logical. But what about the unmade beds?*

Then Dena and Pearl walked in together, not speaking a word, not looking at me.

"Where's Beverly?" I asked.

Dena hung up her robe. "She's gone."

"Home?" I said, then remembered the double meaning of that word at Loon Lake. "You mean, discharged?"

"Yep, discharged." Dena slipped her legs back between the sheets with the speed a hunter might use to slide his knife back into its sheath.

I sat up. "But I didn't—didn't get the chance to say good-bye."

"Join the club," Dena said. "Pearl was right about the discharge order. It just took a while for Beverly's father to get here. And now they've flown this coop!"

Pearl didn't say a word. I expected her to rant and rave or at least pick a fight with Dena. This quiet version of Pearl scared me more than the one who pitched a hissy fit.

Dena, on the other hand, wanted to talk. "We were just starting math when Dr. Tollerud came and ordered Beverly to the main office. We all saw he had the discharge order. Beverly asked if she could say her good-byes. I told her just to go and don't look back. But not Beverly—she didn't move."

My eyes kept skating over Beverly's empty bed, each time expecting to see her round face smiling at me.

"What about her clothes?" I asked. "She can't go home dressed in Loon Lake pajamas!"

"The do-gooders in the Ladies Auxiliary make lots of dresses—for us to wear when we leave or in our coffins," Dena said.

My heart knotted. "What about her other things—the stuff in her drawer?"

Dena pointed to Beverly's now-empty bed and table. "It's cleaned out already. The nurses were too busy doing that to change our sheets."

"I guess I slept through it all," I said, and wiped my eyes on the corner of my sheet. Was I crying because I would miss Beverly, or because I was jealous?

"Fevers will do that to you," Dena told me. "Good thing you slept. You didn't have to watch them scrub down everything Beverly ever breathed on." Dena stared up at the ceiling, her voice ricocheting around the room. "I just hope they don't kill her back on the farm. Seven kids. Beverly will end up taking care of them all."

Our goal had always been to leave Loon Lake, as if just being released could guarantee that we'd never be sick another day of our lives.

"Where's Sarah?" I asked, trying to sound calm. "She missed saying good-bye to Beverly too."

"Getting a pneumo," Dena said with a glance in Pearl's direction. "That is, if you can trust anything Miss Wanda says."

I'd heard Dena's description of a pneumo. Dr. Tollerud stuck a big needle in between her ribs to push air into the space around her lungs. She'd said that if he hit an artery and air got into her brain, she'd go blind or die. What if something bad like that happened to Sarah?

"Hey," said Dena, "being a gas patient isn't so bad. She'll have to drink some rotten medicine before every meal from now on, but since when has medicine ever tasted good?"

I waited for a reaction from Pearl. She didn't get a discharge or a pneumo today—and she'd wanted both so badly. I felt sorry for her—for us all, really. When Pearl didn't explode, I decided she was a better actress than most of those Hollywood stars she read about in her magazines.

Dena fixed her eyes on me until she had my attention. "Sarah will be sore for a couple of days." Dena cocked her head in Pearl's direction, still holding me in her sights. "Give her some time. She'll get over it."

After that, no one talked. Not a single word, as if Beverly had taken our voices with her when she left Loon Lake.

NURSE MARSHALL wheeled Sarah into the room late in the day and shifted her off the gurney and back onto her bed. Sarah didn't open her eyes or signal me. Her limp body—curled up on its side—looked like a question mark.

I studied her sleeping face, as if my eyes—like an X-ray—could tell what was going on inside her lungs. Would the pnuemo help her or not? I didn't know. I wished the answer were as simple as looking up a word in a dictionary.

Later that night, as I thought about all I wanted to tell Sarah, I remembered something Dena had said earlier. Now I needed to know one other thing about Beverly's departure.

"Dena," I asked, trying to whisper loudly enough for her to hear but not so loudly as to wake Sarah. "Did Beverly look back? You know, when she was leaving and you told her to go on and not look back?"

Dena didn't answer at first. When she did finally speak, her voice echoed as if coming from a dark cave, not just from across our room. "Yeah, she looked back. When I go, it's gonna be a clean, surgical cut. No looking back for me. I'll be outta here fast. But not Beverly. She should have been laughing at us and her own good luck, but that girl was crying—crying all the way out of this rotten place."

CHAPTER 22

A Brook

THE HOT WATER BOTTLE bobbed between my feet as I moved it around, hoping to find a new warm spot.

October 25 had finally arrived. That was the day we were allowed to have hot water bottles. Dena and Pearl were off to class and didn't get to enjoy this luxury, but Sarah and I both sighed with pleasure. Oh, to have warm toes again.

Of course, the rest of our bodies remained cold. Windows were kept wide-open almost all the time—the chilly air was supposed to be good for our lungs. Some days were warmer than others, but I almost never woke up now without my teeth chattering.

Sarah grabbed some tissues, then settled back against her pillow. Sometimes, just before our chats, she made a little clicking sound with her tongue to stop the back of her throat from itching. I waited for her to finish. "What were you dreaming about last night, Sarah?"

"I don't remember. Why? Was I talking in my sleep?"

"Yeah, but it didn't make sense. Something about a brook in Illinois?"

"A brook?" Sarah said. But before I could respond her face changed, as if someone had pulled a curtain around her thoughts. "I have a secret, Evvy," she said, speaking so softly I had to lean my head over the edge of my bed to hear. "I promised my parents I wouldn't tell anyone."

"I've never told you any of Abe's secrets. And he has some real doozies. I promise never to tell yours either."

Sarah hesitated, then her face softened. "I was

saying a prayer, asking for God's help. It starts with the Hebrew words *Baruch atah adonai, Eloheinu melech ha' olam'.* Maybe you heard 'brook' and 'Illinois' in that."

"I think I did," I said, hearing her say the strange words again. "Your secret is that you speak Hebrew?"

"No, Evvy," she said, fighting back a smile. "My secret is that I'm Jewish. My real name is Sarah Meier, not Sarah Morgan."

I'd never known a Jewish person before. "Why does it have to be a secret?"

"Because it's not a good time to be Jewish. People think it's okay to blame Jews for everything. Even in America. Even here in Minnesota. Especially if you have TB. My father found a place for me at the Jewish sanatorium in Denver, but my mother didn't want me to be so far away. We were afraid if we told the truth, Loon Lake wouldn't take me. The doctor in St. Paul helped us change my name on the records."

"But no one here would hurt you if they knew you were Jewish." As soon as I said it, I realized someone like Miss Wanda might. I thought for a moment, aware of the extra burden Sarah had been carrying since she arrived. I spoke with more caution. "I promise to keep it a secret, Sarah."

Her eyes flooded me with trust. "I know you will."

But I could see she was still disappointed in

herself, and I had an idea about how to make her feel better. "Could you maybe teach me something about being Jewish? I mean, when no one else is in the room."

She turned her head, her eyes brightening again. "Lesson one, Evvy. Jesus was Jewish."

"He was?" Had I managed to daydream through every important lesson in Sunday school? "I guess I've got a lot to learn."

Sarah smiled. "And you can tell me more about having a twin brother."

I liked the idea of us trying on each other's lives.

The fact that we now shared a secret, an important secret, seemed to hover a moment, then settle like a blanket over both of us.

I reached my hand out. She did the same. Inches separated our fingertips, but it didn't feel that way at all.

October 27, 1940

Dear Evvy,

Still no loons and no lake? Who named that place?

I'm learning to play "Flight of the Bumblebee." Grandma says she hopes the "beezy bee" she keeps hearing will leave some honey soon.

Father needs you in the garden, Ev. I tripped over one of his pumpkun vines. He acted like the German Luftwaffe had dropped bombs on our yard. Gee, only one pumpkun got busted!

School's okay. Mrs. Kittelsby asks about you all the time. She's not such a bad egg after all.

We went to a concert in St. Paul. Father fell asleep. Mother got all weepy over some sad song a lady sang. Not enough trumpet for me. Miss ya.

Your brother,

Abe

PS—Sweetie had her kittens. Five of them. All cute. All claws. I've got the scratches to prove it.

LOON LAKE SANATORIUM

Day Pass
Official Permission Form

Dr. F. H. Tollerud, Medical Director

Pearl Lippert has been granted permission to leave the facility on
(Patient's Name)

November 11 19 _40_ under the supervision of _Edmund Lippert_
(Month and Day)   (Year)   (Responsible Party)

for a period starting no earlier than 8:00 A.M. and ending no later than 8:00 P.M.

Failure to follow Loon Lake guidelines could result in serious consequences. Loon Lake Sanatorium accepts no responsibility for the patient's care off premises.

Authorizing Signatures:

Milton Keith, M.D.
(Attending Physician)

Harriet Marshall, R.N.
(Nurse)

Dr. F.H. Tollerud
(Medical Director)

CHAPTER 23

Cold News

AT LONG LAST Pearl's day with her brother, Edmund, arrived. We all watched as Pearl got dressed in street clothes, her thick hair brushed into waves of curls, her eyes brightened with mascara loaned to her by an older girl. For once, one of us didn't look like a sick patient. Pearl beamed at our attention and promised to bring us all little treats on her return.

Just hours after she left, the weather turned cold. Snow started coming down in a flurry and filling the space between the buildings like flour pouring into a canister.

I tried to make my eyes focus on the book I was reading, *A Rainbow Fills My Sky*. The Loon Lake Library had loaned it to me now that I'd earned reading privileges. But the brave and plucky girl with TB in the story just made me want to empty my sputum cup into a bowl of beef stew.

I decided I'd rather watch the blizzard with Sarah and Dena. But soon the wintry weather made me homesick for Abe. I bet he was already running around outside and flopping down to make snow angels without me.

Was Dena wondering the same thing about her brothers and sisters, or was she an only child like Sarah? I'd never asked Dena about her family before. "Do you have any brothers and sisters, Dena?"

"Two little stepsisters, April and Agnes. They probably wouldn't know me if they walked in the door," she said. "My brother, Michael—Mickey's what I called him—was a year older than me. He got TB too, probably from Pops. Then, when Pops died, Mickey and I got shipped here together. We were on a kids' ward till Mickey went home and I aged up to this room."

A father and brother both lost to TB!

The book fell from my hands and closed with a *fwump*.

"Hey, no need to look like a couple a ghosts, you two." Dena gave a quick wave of her hand, as if that could erase what she'd just told us. "It's not like you knew them or anything."

"But we know you," Sarah said.

"Yeah, but I don't want you or anyone else around this place feeling sorry for me. I told you 'cause you asked. So now we don't need to talk about it anymore. Anyway, I got something else to ask you two."

I picked up the book and put it aside to listen to Dena.

"It's been over a month since Beverly left," she said, "and they haven't tossed a new bug in her bed. TB hasn't exactly dropped off the face of the earth, ya know."

"You haven't heard about anyone coming to take Beverly's place?" Sarah asked.

"Nothing!" Dena said. "And I've been listening. Someone should be in that bed."

Sarah tapped her finger against her cheek. "Maybe . . . Maybe it's not about having new patients at all. Maybe it's something about Loon Lake—"

"Have you noticed," Dena interrupted, "how Old Eagle Eye's been working so many double shifts?"

"Yeah," I groaned, annoyed that Nurse Marshall seemed to be living in our room.

Sarah stopped tapping and looked directly at Dena, the two of them understanding something. "It's not good, is it, Dena? It's Nurse Gunderson. She must be sick."

"Maybe she went home to Winona for a visit?" I said. I didn't want Sarah to be right this time. "Remember she talked about that?"

"Nah, no one around here takes a vacation this long," Dena said. "She didn't leave, and she's not working on another ward either. I bet she's over in the Olson Building, sick just like us."

I tried piecing together what Dena and Sarah must have already realized. Loon Lake couldn't accept new patients if they didn't have enough nurses to take care of them. And hadn't Dr. Keith made some comment about not losing another nurse?

Then a new thought—a worse one—came to me. "Dena, if Nurse Gunderson got sick, was it from us?"

"Probably not. Lots of the doctors and nurses here have TB, or did. Other hospitals don't want to hire 'em. But they can always work at a san."

Sarah didn't look convinced.

Dena kept talking. "Haven't you two ever heard of Dr. Trudeau?" She looked at Sarah, then me. "He's the most famous TB doctor in the whole world. He had the bug too. That's how he figured out rest and fresh air are good for us. He took care of loads of patients."

"I think my father talked about him," Sarah said, putting her thoughts together out loud. "In the Adirondacks—in New York."

"Yep, that's the guy."

I didn't want a medical history lesson right now. "So it's really not our fault she's sick?" I asked Dena again.

For once, she didn't answer with a wisecrack. "Honest. I figure Nurse Gunderson was probably sick before she ever got here."

I remembered Nurse Gunderson falling asleep the night she brought us colas. She'd seemed tired, and even homesick too. Maybe, if she did have TB, that's why she understood us so well.

Then I remembered something else. "I—I think I might have seen Nurse Gunderson's X-ray."

Both girls talked at once. "What?" Sarah said. "Why didn't you tell us this before?" Dena demanded.

"I didn't know what I was seeing." I told them about my first day at Loon Lake and how I overheard Dr. Keith talking to Nurse Marshall. "When Dr. Keith said something about the X-ray being 'one of yours,' I thought he meant it belonged to one of her patients, not to one of her nurses. That probably explains why Dr. Keith sounded so sad that day."

I tried to imagine how I'd feel looking at the sick lungs of someone I loved. I'd never really thought of an X-ray as being a real picture of anyone before— just some hocus-pocus doctors used to prove they were smart and right about everything.

"Do you remember any of the words he said?" Dena asked.

I tried to re-create the scene in my mind's eye. "Lots of medical stuff. I did hear the word *cavitation*. It made me think of cavities and going to the dentist."

"What do you think?" Sarah asked, looking over at Dena.

Dena let her straggly hair hide her face for a moment. Then she shoved it aside and spoke. "Cavitations are like pockets—empty pockets— where healthy lung used to be. We all probably have some. I don't think that means Nurse Gunderson is going to die. But if Dr. Keith is worried, she must be pretty darn sick."

LOON LAKE MENU

NOVEMBER 12, 1940

Today's Food for Thought:

*To weather the weather,
make your own sunshine with a smile.*

BREAKFAST
Oranges
Oatmeal
Scrambled eggs
Dry toast
Canned prunes
Milk, cocoa
Coffee with cream

DINNER
Tomato soup
Boiled chicken
Steamed rice
Fresh spinach
Applesauce
Brown bread, butter
Vanilla pudding
Milk, coffee

SUPPER
Dry cereal
Baked beans
Pork roast
Green salad
Sweet potatoes
Pineapple wedges
Ginger bread, butter
Milk, cocoa, tea

CHAPTER 24

Wind and Weather

"WHO THINKS UP those things?" Sarah said, sounding more annoyed than curious.

"You mean the menu?" I could see she was reading the sheet of paper that came with our food trays.

"No, the little 'Food for Thought' at the top," Sarah answered. "Like today's: 'To weather the weather, make your own sunshine with a smile.'"

Dena set up a game of solitaire on her tray table. "Probably the same Pollyannas who write the *Loon Lake Booster*."

We were all cranky, and not just because of worry over Nurse Gunderson. Pearl had not come back yesterday, and if it got much later, she wouldn't be back today either. The blizzard seemed to have upset everything, as if we were stuck upside down in an overturned snow globe.

"And will ya both quit worrying about Pearl!" Dena said, smacking a card on the tray. "She hit the jackpot. Thanks to all this snow, she gets an extra day away from this place. And we get an extra day of peace and quiet without her."

Sarah rolled the top edge of her blanket back and forth under her hands. I picked my way through another awful book. I'd have to make Abe promise to send me a good book to read—the gorier the better!

The day dragged on and on, and so did the night. It was still dark when I heard footsteps in our room and then the door swishing closed. A voice squealed, "I saw it, I saw it! Wake up! I have to tell you all about it. I got to see *Gone with the Wind*!"

Pearl was back in her pajamas and gushing with excitement as she slipped into bed. I fluffed my pillow and mumbled hello. Dena pulled the covers over her head and muttered, "Just my luck."

"Glad you're safe," Sarah said with a yawn.

"Of course I'm safe," Pearl bragged. "I was with Edmund. The whole state is shut down—some places had twenty-five inches of snow with drifts practically up to the moon—but Edmund was prepared. He already had the knobbies on his car."

"Knobbies?" Sarah asked, curious even at this time of night.

"You know, special tires for snow." Pearl paused for a second in her own blizzard of words. "Once the plows went through, Edmund and I were the first people back on the road. But I don't want to talk about some stupid snowstorm," Pearl said, flapping her hands like little wings. "*Gone with the Wind* is such a swell movie!"

"Ah, here we go," Dena said with a groan, her head emerging from under the blankets. "That wind isn't gone yet." But then she kept quiet and let Pearl do all the talking.

Pearl told us about nearly every scene in the long movie. And when she finished with that, she told us about her brother, Edmund, and how he'd promised next time to take her to visit her best friend, Muriel.

"Oh, and I've got presents for you," Pearl said, still bubbling with excitement. She got out of bed, flipped on the bathroom light so we could see—not well, but enough—and handed each of us a folding paper fan. "Open them," she said.

Dena started to chuckle. Then we all laughed when we saw her fan had a dragon on it. "Pretty good, Pearl."

Mine had a fish on it. "Because you can stand to drink cod-liver oil!" Pearl said.

I smiled, pleased that she'd noticed. "Thanks."

I'm not sure Pearl heard me, because she was already talking to Sarah. "Yours has a fancy scroll like a college diploma on it."

Sarah smiled and gave the fan a gentle wave to show it off.

Pearl reached into a bag and pulled out others. "I didn't know what to get for Nurse Marshall," she said, holding another fan up to the light, "so I got an ocean scene."

"Probably has a crab in it somewhere," Dena joked.

"And for Nurse Gunderson I got one with a white horse." We all oohed and ahhed as we admired the perfect gift for our favorite nurse. "I had Edmund mail one with chickens on it to Beverly—you know, because she lives on a farm—and he sent one with a beautiful lady in a fancy gown to Muriel. I just know she'll love it."

"Thank you," I said again, this time so Pearl heard me.

"You're welcome—all of you." Pearl looked over at Dena. "Don't you want to know what fan I got for myself?"

"They put movie stars on those things?" Dena asked.

Pearl smiled. "Not exactly." She opened up the last fan. A beautiful peacock spread its tail across the rippling folds of the white paper.

"Now, that's swell, Pearl. Real swell," Dena said.

Sarah and I had to agree. We all closed up our fans and put them away in our bedside drawers. Then Pearl leaned back onto her bed and sighed in her dramatic way.

Dena got up and shut off the bathroom light. By the time she was back in bed, Pearl was already fast asleep, the soft huffs and puffs of her breathing as familiar to me now as my own.

November 13, 1940

Dear Grandma Hoffmeister,

   I'm glad you took care of Mr. Arendt's
dog during the big Armistice Day
blizzard! I'm sure Trapper liked your
homemade stew. I didn't know they're
calling that storm the Winds of Hell.
Even the Lutherans?

   I thought you might like to hear our
own Armistice Day story.

   Pearl went to town with her older
brother and got caught in the big storm.
Don't worry, she's okay. She brought
us all back folding paper fans and
everybody got one with a different
design. Mine has a fish on it since,
thanks to you, I'm the only one
around here who doesn't mind taking
cod-liver oil.

                                    →

We sometimes open the fans when we have our hot milk before bedtime. We nicknamed Pearl "president of the fan club." She likes that.

So I guess we did have an armistice here too—our own little peace.

Love,
Evvy

CHAPTER 25

A Ruby

I'D JUST LEFT the bathroom, taking advantage of my latest and best privilege, when I heard a scream—or really, felt it—coming from out in the hallway. I looked back at Sarah, whose frantic eyes pushed me out the door to see what had happened.

I'd never actually stood in the corridor before. My view had always been from a wheelchair, so my sense of size and distance felt muddled and dizzying.

Then Nurse Marshall swept by me, ordering another nurse to call Dr. Tollerud immediately. People clogged the long hallway.

Another scream seemed to peel off into words.

"Help! Someone, help!"

I recognized Dena's voice; my eyes searched for her in the confusion. *Please God, not Dena, not her too, not after her father and brother.*

"Get a stretcher," another voice yelled.

"It's a hemorrhage!" More voices all talking at once.

I slid along the wall, pulled by a current of fear into darker waters.

Up ahead a young nurse stopped moving and looked down.

My eyes followed hers. Was that Dena's dark hair I saw? Was someone else there too?

Dr. Tollerud rushed by, sputtering commands. The still-frozen nurse blocked me from seeing more.

I heard a faint gurgling sound. The nurse seemed to wake to Dr. Tollerud's orders and step aside.

Then I could see. Dena was on the floor clutching Pearl.

Pearl—but not Pearl.

Bright red blood covered her body. It ran like ribbons through her brown curls. It trailed in thin streams down her arms and onto her robe. It bubbled a too-brilliant red at her mouth.

"Fight, Pearl, fight," Dena pleaded.

Patients from other rooms crowded around, stepping closer, whispering, pointing.

Dena looked up and snarled, "Give her some breathing room!"

I pushed to get through, but others pushed back harder. I leaned around a bystander's arm and saw Pearl's head drop forward, then hinge back.

An orderly with a gurney scattered the crowd. Dr. Tollerud and Nurse Marshall dragged Pearl's limp, bloodied body from Dena's arms and up onto the gurney's pad.

Then they raced down the hall. Dr. Keith appeared and ran alongside as they turned into an examining room.

"Looks like she threw a ruby," another person said.

"She's a goner," someone mumbled.

"Get back to your beds. Show's over," a staff member instructed.

People scuttled away. Had someone said she'd hemorrhaged? Thrown a ruby?

Somehow Sarah appeared at my side, her feather-light body pressed against mine, her large eyes gathering in the scene.

Dena, still holding on to Pearl's bloody robe, crouched on the floor in front of us.

"Dena," I said, "I'm here—we're here."

Dena raised her head, then took my arm and stood up. The three of us, accompanied by a nurse, made our way like tired soldiers back to our room.

As I crawled into bed, I turned to ask the nurse

about Pearl, but the weary look on her face already told me all I needed to know.

We'd lost Pearl.

I didn't try to hold back my tears; Sarah didn't either.

And the nurse didn't tell us to stop crying. She tucked the blanket around my shaking shoulders, and did the same for Sarah. Then she tended to Dena, washing away Pearl's blood and hanging up both robes. When the nurse finished, she looked at each of us a moment before lowering her head and leaving the room.

As soon as the door closed, Dena pushed off the blankets and sat up. "TB didn't kill her. Muriel's mother did!"

"What? Wait—don't, Dena," I said. "Not right now."

She ignored me. I turned to look at Sarah, afraid she'd have her hands over her ears, afraid she couldn't take any more, afraid I couldn't either.

But Sarah wasn't looking at me. She lifted her head, wiped her eyes on a corner of her blanket, and spoke to Dena. "She had a hemoptysis, Dena—a hemorrhage. Maybe the trip with Edmund was too much for her, or the cold, or the—"

"Yeah, the doctors and nurses are gonna tell us

that. They got lots of answers, but big words aren't the same as truth."

"But the bloo—"

"Look, Sarah, tuberculosis can kill ya a hundred—no, a thousand—different ways. Rot out your lungs, go into your bones, eat through your guts, turn your brain to oatmeal. Consume you."

Dena waved her hand in the air, then went on. "I know Pearl threw a ruby, knew it as soon as it happened. I didn't see Pops die, but they say he hemorrhaged that way too. TB ate right through his lung and into an artery. But it's not just the bug that kills ya."

My head hurt and my heart ached. "Dena, can't this wait?"

"Let her talk," Sarah said. "She knows more."

New tears filled my eyes. I could almost hear the rest of Sarah's thought: *than you do, Evvy*. Didn't Sarah understand that nothing Dena could say would bring Pearl back?

Dena grumbled as she dropped her head into her hands. "I'll tell you what killed her. All her dreaming to be something—anything—but a lunger."

Dena kept talking without looking up at either of us. "On the way back from class, Pearl saw some mail—a letter to her, right on top. No one was looking, so she grabbed it, all excited 'cause she could tell it was from Muriel's mother.

"'I'm just sure she wants to invite me to their holiday party or maybe to their lake house next summer,' Pearl squealed while she opened that stupid envelope. I wished I'd yanked it right out of her hands."

"What did it say?" Sarah asked, now with a tremble in her voice.

Dena got out of bed and went to Pearl's robe. She pulled a fancy note card out of the robe's pocket and handed it to Sarah.

"Just enough to break that foolish girl's heart."

November 17, 1940

Dear Pearl,

Muriel was delighted to receive the little gift you purchased for her. You two have always been such sweet friends and cared so much about each other. That is why I know you'll understand that for Muriel's sake and good health, we think it best you two not see each other in the future. No doctor can guarantee a complete cure for consumption, and, as Muriel's dear friend, you would never want her to suffer as you have.

We trust you will respect our wishes.

Mrs. Robert Banlow

CHAPTER 26

A Different Current

PEARL DIED November 20, the day before Thanksgiving. No one felt like celebrating. The turkey and stuffing we'd all been looking forward to eating together went untouched on our plates. Dena pointed out that it wasn't really Thanksgiving anyway. "Just because President Roosevelt made the holiday a week earlier doesn't make it right." I remembered Father explaining to Abe and me last year how the president was trying to help businesses by giving people an extra week between Thanksgiving and Christmas to shop. But I had to agree with Dena—the holiday just didn't feel right. Especially now.

Then, a few days after Thanksgiving, a letter arrived from Beverly. Nurse Marshall brought it to our room but said nothing as she handed it to Dena. We all thought it was about what happened, but it wasn't. It was a thank-you note to Pearl for the fan she'd sent.

"I'd better write and tell Beverly," Dena told us.

"Not alone, Dena," I said. "We'll do it together."

And the three of us did. Even though I liked playing with words, and Sarah was a crackerjack student, I think Dena said it best:

Pearl could be a pain. But so is everything else here. I wish she hadn't died.

The last week of November brought other changes to our room—some small, some important.

Dena started sleeping more, even during the Cure Hour. She joked that the bright light hurt her eyes, but I didn't buy that; she was tired and worn out by what had happened, and so were we. As for Sarah, she asked Dena fewer questions now. At first I thought this was good, but then I wasn't so sure. Sarah seemed happier when she was curious, and sadder now that she wasn't. Her dark eyes brightened only when we talked. I told her stories about Abe or sometimes Grandma Hoffmeister. "Your family is such fun," she said with envy in her voice. "My parents are such worriers—and all they worry about is me!" Maybe being an only child and getting all the attention wasn't so great after all. As for me, I had restless dreams, as if someone had screamed "Emergency!" just before I woke up. I'd rub my eyes and feel like I was supposed to be doing something. But there was nothing to be done.

Then the biggest change happened. On December 1, Sarah was taken from our room—we thought to get a pneumo treatment. But when she didn't come back by evening, we knew something else was going on. I spent half my time imagining the worst, the other half hounding Dena to find out news for us.

A day and a half later, Dena dropped a crumpled piece of paper on my bed. "Someone handed me this."

I looked at the words "Tell Eve I'm like Adam" and saw a drawing of a simple clockface. I recognized Sarah's handwriting at once.

"It's from Sarah," I said, pleased to be the Eve of her message.

Dena sat down on the edge of my bed. "Yeah, I figured, but what does it mean?"

I read the message again, this time as if Sarah were inside my head, coaching me. *Think about Adam.* "Dena, isn't there some operation where they remove a rib?"

"Sure, it's called a thoracoplasty. The doctors pull

out a rib—or a couple of them—and collapse the lung to let it heal."

I thought again, then handed the message back to Dena. "I think Sarah had a thoracoplasty. That's how she's like Adam from the Bible—losing a rib."

"Yeah, I get it now," Dena said, looking at the note. "Pretty smart, *Eve*-vy."

I wasn't sure who Dena thought was smart— Sarah for thinking it up or me for solving it.

Dena arched an eyebrow in my direction. "One of the old-timers around here has had eleven of his ribs cut out."

"Eleven?! How many ribs do people have to begin with?"

"Twenty-four, twelve on each side," Dena answered. "Don't worry, Evvy. It took 'em a long time to take all those ribs out."

I wondered how a person would look without one rib, let alone eleven. "How come he doesn't just bend in two without ribs to hold him up?"

"'Cause he always wears some gizmo strapped around his chest for support."

"Like a brassiere?" I said, blushing as I remembered the lopsided man I'd seen on my first day at Loon Lake.

Dena chuckled. "Yeah, I guess, but don't tell *him* that."

"I won't," I promised, then pointed back to Sarah's note. "But why the clock?"

Dena looked more closely at Sarah's little drawing. "One eighteen—that's just before the Cure Hour starts."

"Or maybe," I said with a sudden sense of knowing, "it's her new room number."

"Yeah, could be a private room." Dena started to go to her bed, then paused and said, "Ya know, Evvy, maybe it's better that's she's not in our room for a while."

Had I heard Dena right? "What?" I asked. "Why?"

Dena turned to face me. "I don't see her getting well with you two talking all the time."

"So it's my fault Sarah's sick? Is that what you think?" It was one thing to have Nurse Marshall get after me, but something altogether different to have Dena telling me how to behave. "You're the one always barking about the stupid rules around here!"

"Yeah, the rules are stupid, but so are people sometimes. Maybe if you'd let Sarah rest once in a while, she'd have half a chance to get better!"

I stood and snatched Sarah's note from her hands. "And maybe"—I felt something coming untied inside me—"maybe you'd understand, Dena, if you'd ever had a best friend!"

Dena narrowed her eyes. "You don't understand

any—" She stopped midsentence, then dropped her empty hands in disgust. "Forget it," she said. "Just forget it!" She moved away from me, as if our anger had become as contagious as our disease.

My shoulders slumped. I stared down at Sarah's note. The little face on her hand-drawn clock seemed to look up at me disapprovingly. "I'm sorry," I mumbled.

Dena got up and walked over to her bedside table and opened the drawer. She came back, her mouth cutting a straight line across her face, and handed me a picture. "That's my brother, Mickey—my best friend."

I studied the photo of a boyish face like Dena's. He had a scruff of hair and a playful look in his eye that seemed devilish and friendly at once. "You two look more alike than Abe and me, and we're twins."

She took back the photo, her face unchanged. "They kept us next to each other when we got to Loon Lake. Over on the little kids' ward. I made Mickey promise we'd stick together no matter what. So at night, we'd hold hands. That way they couldn't take one of us away without waking the other one up."

Could Dena know I woke up at night sometimes to check on Sarah?

"I kept telling Mickey we'd fight this together. I didn't want to see how he was getting sicker and sicker. Even more of a runt than me."

Dena didn't look at me or the photo. "I was

holding Mickey's hand when he died. Nothing I did kept him alive. Nothing."

For a moment, Mickey's face blurred into Pearl's in my mind. I wished I didn't remember the Pearl slumped in Dena's arms—only the one reading her movie magazines or telling us about *Gone with the Wind*. But the broken Pearl and the broken Mickey somehow fit together now, joined by Dena's hand into one memory for me.

"At least you tried, Dena—more than anyone else."

"Maybe, but maybe for the wrong reasons. I wanted to be the big hero, Evvy, the one who could save Mickey when the doctors and everyone else failed." Now she looked straight at me. "I couldn't save him. Or Pearl either."

I wiped tears on my pajama sleeve. "So we just give up. Is that it?"

"Now, that's funny, Evvy. Me quitting? That's sure not going to happen. I'm just learning, that's all. Look, if Mickey or Pearl or Marianne had lived, could I take the credit?" She answered her own question with a shake of her head. "I'd be just another jackass like Dr. Tollerud or Nurse Marshall. They don't have all the answers. If they did, maybe they'd take the blame once in a while. You'll never see that happen around here."

Dena paused, her voice dropping to a rough whisper. "If something happened to Sarah, how do you think you'd feel, Evvy?"

My heart stumbled.

"You'd feel lousy. Like I did about Mickey."

Dena was right, though her words stung. Just because Sarah wanted to talk and be with me too wouldn't make me feel any better if something terrible happened.

"I beat myself up about that for a long time," Dena said. "Maybe even took some of it out on Pearl."

I looked over to where Sarah should have been resting, then back at Dena. "I guess we shouldn't talk at all, then."

"Nah, Evvy," Dena said with a laugh. "That'd be like trying to cork a volcano. Just use some common sense. Take care of yourself, and let Sarah take care of herself too. Help her by not helping so much."

I folded Sarah's note and put it in my drawer, alongside the fan from Pearl, and thought about how Mother used to find ways to separate Abe and me. "Just because you and Abe can rely on each other all the time," she'd say, "doesn't mean you should. You've got to learn to stand on your own two feet."

Now Dena was trying to teach me the same lesson, only this time about Sarah.

I felt a strange shiver inside, as if an old wire had been cut and a new one was starting to send a different current through me.

Could I really stand on my own—just Evvy, instead of Evvy *and* someone else? Could I ever be that strong? Even when Sarah came back? Even without Dena here to remind me once she moved up to the adult ward?

I wasn't sure, but for now I listened to us both breathe. In and out, in and out—a steady rhythm. Like the sound of Mother's metronome on our piano back home, with its thin arm swaying back and forth, setting the tempo for one of her music students.

Now I imagined it measuring our breaths. In and out, in and out.

That was my music—our music—now.

DECEMBER 1940

SUNDAY	MONDAY	TUESDAY	WEDNESDAY	THURSDAY	FRIDAY	SATURDAY
1	2	3	4	5	6	7
8	9	10	11	12	13	14
15	16	17	18	19	20	21
22	23	24 HANUKKAH BEGINS AT SUNSET	25 CHRISTMAS	26	27	28
29	30	31				

CHAPTER 27

Gifts

I TRIED TO get into the holiday spirit, but my letters home must have let on how I was really feeling since my family sent my gifts almost two weeks early. I was glad to get them. But until I actually held those presents in my hands, I hadn't realized how much I'd secretly been hoping to be discharged by Christmas. I knew I wasn't fully well yet, and I wouldn't want to leave until Sarah was better, but still. . . .

I was glad Abe had picked out the book *A Tale of Two Cities* to give me. He figured correctly that reading about heads being chopped off in the French Revolution would cheer me up much more than hearing about carefree children having their wishes come true. Father had sent me a collection of crossword puzzles, though I knew I'd need Sarah's help to finish them all, especially with the harder clues about geography.

Grandma Hoffmeister had sent me not a book but a new 1941 calendar with old-fashioned scenes from around Minnesota at the top of each month. She'd written across the front cover in her heavy black pen: "Watch the time to fly by!" The word "to" was crossed out, which made me think Abe had pointed out she didn't need it.

The calendar also included two extra months: December 1940 and January 1942. I discovered something curious in looking at the December page: Christmas Day this year happened to coincide with Hanukkah.

Sarah had told me a little about Hanukkah, the Jewish Festival of Lights—how it lasted eight days, and that it wasn't the most important Jewish holiday but, because it usually fell near Christmas, people paid more attention to it. She'd also explained that Hanukkah wasn't on the same date every year because the original Hebrew calendar didn't match up with our modern one.

But I liked the idea that our two holidays shared

the same day this year. I wondered if Sarah knew, and hoped somehow she did.

To my surprise, of all the books in my holiday gift box, the one I found myself reading most was Mother's gift, a book of poems. Abe had probably complained about her choice—reading was one thing, but reading poetry would be harsh punishment in his mind. But if he did try to talk her out of the idea, I was glad Mother didn't listen. The book was small and thin with a green cover and sat nicely in my hand. At first I made a game of thinking up a word—a fancy poetic word like "lament" or "twilight" or "dwell"—and skimming along until I found that word, then reading the whole poem. "Dwell" was a really good one, since people in poems dwelled—not lived—in houses, and lots of poets had pain or sadness dwelling in their breasts. I knew how that felt.

An even bigger surprise was that Dena liked me to read the poems aloud to her. She didn't say that exactly, but whenever I reached for the book, she'd point at it, then herself, and tip her head back to listen.

In turn, she worked to find out about Sarah. Sarah was sitting up now and feeding herself—that was the good news—but she was alone in a small room with nothing more than a tree outside her window to keep her company.

An idea edged its way into my thoughts. I knew what I had to do.

The real question was whether I should tell Dena my plan or not.

CHAPTER 28

More Gifts

ON DECEMBER 23, Dr. Keith gave me an early present: "You can be up for three hours a day and no longer need to use a wheelchair." He put his notes in my chart, then added, "Also, you will be attending classes and Activity in January."

I wanted to cheer, but I settled for a thumbs-up from Dena and the secret thought that my plan would be easier to carry out now that I had permission to walk.

I knew my family would be happy too. Abe might laugh that I saw going to school as a reward, but he would be glad to know I was doing better. This was the best gift—really the only gift—I could give them for Christmas.

I hurried to write my family and each of my grandmothers so the letters could go out with the next mail. I needed to keep myself busy anyway, or else I'd start feeling homesick or worried about carrying out my plan. Plus, I wanted to cover the envelopes with the Christmas seals Grandma Hoffmeister had enclosed in her last letter—my way of letting her know the money she'd spent may have done me and others some good.

Christmas morning we awoke to carolers—a group of doctors and nurses roving up and down the hall, singing. Though all were dressed in their regular hospital whites, some had added colorful scarves, others donned knit hats, and Nurse Marshall—yes, our Nurse Marshall!—wore floppy, Santa-sized boots on her feet. Dr. Tollerud himself wore a red pointed cap and conducted the singers with a wave of a large candy cane.

Applause mingled with coughs when they sang the final note of "Good King Wenceslas" and left with a jingle of sleigh bells.

"Now, that's a Christmas miracle," Dena said. "Seeing them having fun!"

But the warm holiday glow faded along with the last jingle. I wished I'd made something for Dena for Christmas. I pulled open my drawer, as if some perfect little present might be waiting there for me to give her.

Instead I stared at the fan from Pearl and remembered something else.

"Dena, what happened to the fan Pearl bought for Nurse Gunderson?"

"I swiped it," Dena said matter-of-factly. "I didn't want Miss Wanda taking it, so I stuck it in my drawer for safekeeping."

"I'm glad," I said, then pointed to Sarah's bedside table. "Sarah's still got hers."

"Yeah, I know. I checked too."

A sad feeling seemed to fill the room, as if we'd both reached the bottom of our Christmas stockings and still hadn't found what we'd hoped for.

"Dena?"

She looked up at me, her bangs hanging dark over her eyes.

"Would you maybe—I mean, would you want to do a fan club again?"

I knew it was silly to ask. Even when Pearl was alive, all we did was open our fans, wave them about, laugh, and drink our milk or hot chocolate together.

Dena answered by opening her drawer. She lifted her fan and spread it open, her own head directly above the dragon's. I had to laugh at the sight.

"Yeah, I know," Dena said, laughing with me. "This is my real twin."

CHAPTER 29

The Plan

FINALLY, WE WERE on our way to the dining hall for our special Christmas dinner. I took a few steps on tiptoe, then some long strides to test out my legs, until Dena said, "Cut out the ballet and just walk." But I couldn't help myself. I was just so glad to be moving on my own and not in a wheelchair.

We stepped into a hall decorated with green boughs and gold ribbon, silver stars and poinsettias, and a brightly lit Christmas tree in the corner.

"Merry Christmas!" Dena said, more as a comment than a greeting.

Tree at My Window
by
Robert Frost

Then she poked me with an elbow. "Check to see if she's here. She might be well enough to come to dinner."

"Sarah?" I said as my eyes swept the room.

"Not Sarah," Dena corrected me. "Nurse Gunderson."

I looked for them both. "It might help if everyone around here didn't wear white!" Then I had an idea. "Look for Dr. Keith. We should be able to spot his hair easily enough, and I bet he'll have her nearby."

We both kept an eye out but didn't spot Dr. Keith, Nurse Gunderson, or Sarah.

I ate everything on my plate, probably too fast, and managed to get gravy on my sleeve in my hurry to be finished. At last the dishes got cleared, and the nurse at our table slid her chair back and sipped a cup of coffee in the leisurely way Father might on a quiet evening back home. Several of the orderlies pushed a piano into the room through the large double doors, and I saw a woman setting up some music stands alongside it. Folded cards on the table told us that after a concert of holiday music, dessert would be served.

Now was my chance. People were still busy clearing the tables, and if I was lucky, no one would notice or care if I went off to the bathroom.

I caught the nurse's eye and got permission, then made my way out the door. I felt bad not telling Dena the truth, but someone would have noticed two of us leaving.

Outside in the hallway, more people were bustling about. One woman was carrying a violin; a man had his arm wrapped around a cello like it was his date. No one paid any attention to me.

I headed toward the bathroom but turned down another hallway instead, thinking if anyone stopped me, I'd pretend to be lost.

I scooted along the wall and watched as the numbers on each door told me I was getting closer to what I hoped was Sarah's room. My cheeks felt flushed, my neck warm. Was that from nervousness? Excitement? Too much exercise? I couldn't worry about that now. Not when I was at her door.

I paused. What if they'd moved her and I didn't get to see her? What if this wasn't her room?

I took a deep breath and stepped inside. Sarah was resting, her eyes closed, her bed facing the window. I glanced to see her tree. A few brown leaves still trembled on the branches as if trying to hold on despite the wind and snow.

I tiptoed to her bed and took out the gift I'd tucked under my bathrobe. It was a poem copied from my new green book. I hadn't wanted to write

"Happy Hanukkah" at the top for fear of revealing Sarah's secret. But I had drawn lots of small blue six-sided stars—the kind Sarah called the Star of David—to decorate the edge of the paper, then added a half moon as an afterthought. I hadn't signed my name—she would know it was from me. I reached over to slide it under her pillow.

I wanted to wake her, to see her change from this pale, sick girl back into Sarah. I didn't want to go without at least saying hello. But I knew I shouldn't. Just as I stepped away, she twisted in bed, lifting one shoulder up off the sheet, and woke up. Her eyes froze on me with a startled look.

"Evvy!" she called in a thin voice, and reached for my arm.

She was awake! Bandages crinkled as she moved.

"I came to wish you a happy Hanukkah, Sarah," I whispered.

For a moment we just looked at each other—tired and excited, worried and relieved, miserable and thankful, but at least together.

A flicker of excitement lit her marble-dark eyes. "It is Hanukkah! And Christmas too. Merry Christmas, Evvy."

"Happy Hannukah to you, Sarah. I brought you something." I pointed under her pillow. "You can read it later."

I had to go. I knew every second away increased my chances of getting caught. Dena would be right to call me foolish—or even worse—if I didn't leave right now and let Sarah rest.

"Don't go, Evvy," Sarah said, grabbing my arm. "Not yet."

I sat down on her bed, slumped like a marionette, waiting for someone to pull my strings one direction or the other.

"Okay, just a little longer."

She gave a nervous smile, then pressed a handkerchief to her lips, muffling her voice as she spoke. "I can't do this, Evvy—not on my own."

"You don't have to do it on your own forever. Just get well enough to come back to our room."

The handkerchief dropped, and worry still showed on her face.

"They wouldn't leave your things in our room if they weren't planning on moving you back. That's what Dena thinks too."

Sarah listened, but didn't seem convinced.

"You can't give up, Sarah. You just can't."

Sarah watched me out of the corner of her eyes, as if from that angle she could reach deeper inside me to find something she could believe.

"Dena's got me following the rules these days. She thinks that's the best thing we can do for each other—take care of ourselves and get well. I'm even drinking all my buttermilk now. Why, I'm almost a Pollyanna!"

"Almost," Sarah said, letting a little grin slide across her face. "Except for sneaking out to come see me."

"Yep, except for that."

Sarah smiled, her eyes brightening. "Well, then, you'd better get going before they find you, Pollyanna."

I stood up and hoped Sarah didn't notice how my legs wobbled. "Just promise me you'll try to get better, Sarah."

"I promise. And you promise too." She waved me away.

I willed my feet to move forward and didn't look back for fear I wouldn't be able to leave.

But I did.

I eased my way out the door and right into Dr. Keith's white jacket.

CHAPTER 30

The Lie

"EVVY," DR. KEITH said, looking down into my surprised face, "what are you doing here?"

My mind went blank. I couldn't lie, but I couldn't tell the truth.

Then he glanced around and saw Sarah's door.

"I think I understand," he said, then placed his hand on my arm and guided me down the corridor. "You should not have done this, Evvy." His deep voice sounded stern, though he called me Evvy, not Evelyn.

"I'm sorry" was the best I could mumble as I tried to keep up with his pace. "I just had to see—"

"Not another word," he warned me as we turned down a hallway.

Is he going to send me home? Even if Abe and Father could forgive me, I didn't think Mother ever would.

My palms went clammy, and I had to work to keep my feet moving. Dr. Keith must have decided to hand me over to Nurse Marshall.

We turned down the next corridor, and off in the distance I could hear music. We were heading back toward the dining hall, just by a different way.

The music got louder and closer. A Christmas carol, "Silent Night."

Then a sharp voice called down the corridor; in an instant an arm plucked me from his side.

"There you are!" Nurse Marshall said with a triumphant stomp of her heel. She yanked me in her direction. "I should have known better, Dr. Keith," she said. "Even on Christmas I am fully responsible for these girls. I should never have let this one get out of my sight!" Nurse Marshall held on tight to my arm, as if I might bolt again any second.

My head dropped—I knew what Dr. Keith was about to say.

Was that a tremble I felt in Nurse Marshall's fingers as we both waited for Dr. Keith to speak? Could my disappearing act get her in trouble too?

Dr. Keith gave Nurse Marshall a polite smile. "On the contrary, the responsibility belongs entirely to me."

"But Dr. Keith," I protested, not wanting him to take the blame for my adventure.

"No need to talk, Evelyn," he said, calling me by my full name. "I'm the one at fault here. I should have let Nurse Marshall know I needed your assistance briefly with some of the younger children—it being Christmas and all."

I couldn't believe what I was hearing. Dr. Keith was lying on my behalf.

"Well, then, merry Christmas to you, Dr. Keith," she said as she hurried me back into the dining hall.

I sat down just in time to join the others for a dish of peppermint ice cream.

Dena harrumphed under her breath to get my attention, but as long as Nurse Marshall hovered nearby, I kept a stunned smile—however forced—on my face. I needed to be the perfect Pollyanna now.

And I was, until Dena leaned over and whispered, "So, how's Sarah doing?"

I dropped my spoon and splattered ice cream all down the front of my robe.

POEMS
FOR
EVERY MOOD

COMPILED BY
HARRIET MONROE
AND
MORTON DAUWEN ZABEL

CHAPTER 31

Making Sense

AFTER SEEING SARAH, I felt like I'd inched my way out of our white cocoon of a room only to have to crawl right back in again. In my restlessness, I found myself reading more poems from the book Mother gave me, then starting to write some of my own.

I'd always thought making up a poem would be easy—just slap a couple of words together, maybe rhyme a few, and be done. But now that I tried, I could see it was much harder than that. Though the words seemed to glide through my head during the Cure Hour, once I sat up to write them, they just clunked along.

Sometimes I painted myself into a corner, coming up with a line I liked—*The cold night blows a lonely dust*—but not liking any line that I could think of to follow: *Winter wears a frosty crust* or *My shoulders tremble with each gust*. But sometimes the lines seemed to click together like puzzle pieces.

I still read poems aloud to Dena and tried to pay more attention to how they were put together. Some poems seemed to be built with blocks, each verse shaped like the last but adding another level to the tower of words. Other poems felt woven, with lines of different colors, until the overall design appeared.

I'd once offered to read stories to Dena instead. "Nah, stick to poems," she said. "They don't waste time trying to make sense. They just do. That's better for around here."

So I stuck to poetry, reading and writing it, and adding a little color to our cocoon.

WELCOME TO ACTIVITY

Need a matron's help?

No cause to talk,
You will be seen—
Just turn your card
From gray to green!

Then, when the matron
Steps away,
Just turn your card
From green to gray!

Instead of
knitting up your brow,
learn to knit—
we'll show you how!

DON'T COUNT THE DAYS:
MAKE EVERY DAY
COUNT FOR YOUR CURE!

A busy hand,
A carefree heart
Will give your lungs
A healthy start!

Remember . . .
A cheerful face
makes a cheerful place!
So let's all smile!

Now that you're a busy bee
Buzzing through Activity,
Be kind to others and yourself:
A honey heart is sweet for health!

DON'T FORGET . . .
NO TALKING ALLOWED!!
(OR ALOUD!!)

CHAPTER 32

A Warning

"JANELLE'S THE WORST YET!" Dena told me as we headed downstairs for my first Activity. "It's like living with a bagpipe!"

I agreed. Janelle was the new girl in our room. She'd arrived with the new year and she had hardly stopped crying since. She sobbed in fits of such force that I worried she might actually inhale the thermometer this morning. But after listening to her, I wished she would.

I had tried offering her some reassuring words her first night in our room. She'd sat up and screamed that her father would be coming soon to take her back home and we were never, ever to speak to her again. That would be easy.

"It's a relief to get out of the room," I said, letting Dena guide me down one hallway and onto the next.

Getting to the outdoor pavilion for my first class yesterday had been even trickier. I was bundled up in an oversized coat and forced to wear what Nurse Marshall called a "woolen helmet" on my head. Not only did it itch, it limited my vision. Dena had to grab my arm and set me back on course more than once as we trudged through the biting cold. I did learn that our teacher, Mr. Blandiss, had been a student at Carleton College—which pleased me, since we lived only a few blocks from the school in Northfield. Unfortunately, I also discovered that, frozen or thawed, I was still lousy at geometry.

"Go on in," Dena said, opening the door to the Activity room for me. I stepped inside and paused. After months of staring at white walls from my bed, this room with dozens of people at work seemed a beehive of activity. Groups of girls sat at various tables, each working on a project. Some were knitting, some weaving on wooden looms, some hooking pot holders, and others sewed buttons onto the hospital pajamas while still others worked on the *Loon Lake Booster*. Everyone was a busy—but quiet—bee. No one laughed or talked—not allowed, I realized from reading posters on the wall.

Three Activity matrons kept a watchful eye on us all. I tried knitting first. An older girl showed me the basics and got me started. Then she went back to her own knitting. Her needles clicked so fast, her ball of yarn seemed to hop for fear of being turned into a sweater. My yarn, by contrast, appeared to be hibernating and hardly moved at all. After three uneven rows, I lost interest.

As instructed by the signs on the wall, I took the gray card resting on the table and turned it over to the green side. The Activity matron reluctantly acknowledged me, and I soon sat down in front of an old, battered Underwood typewriter. At first I pecked out one letter after the next, slowly and carefully. Then I lost patience and pounded too fast. The little silver bars that held the letters locked up like miniature swords caught in a duel. So I had to go back to tap, tap, tapping. I could tell from the stares of some of the other girls that my typing was as annoying to them as Janelle's sobs were to me.

But that didn't stop me, especially once I got the idea to write Sarah a note. She needed to be warned about bagpipe Janelle and to know I was an Up Patient now. So I typed a message with as many cross-outs as my math homework usually had. Then Dena figured out a way to get my letter to Sarah. Two days later Dena brought a note back for me.

Dear E,

　　I heard an orderly tell Miss W that Nurse G has her name on a box and is going to be in it soon.

　　Please help her like you helped me.

Love,
S

I knew the box had to be a coffin, and that meant Nurse Gunderson must be really sick. But just because Sarah thought my visit had helped her didn't mean I could do anything for Nurse Gunderson.

Somehow, though, I knew Sarah didn't see it that way. She believed in me, and that's all I really needed to know.

I folded Sarah's note on the way to class. "Did you read it, Dena?"

She slowed and nodded her head.

I stopped alongside her and scrunched up my shoulders from the cold. "I'm going to take Nurse Gunderson the fan from Pearl," I said all in one breath.

Dena took hold of my arm and looked me in the eyes. "Then I'm going too."

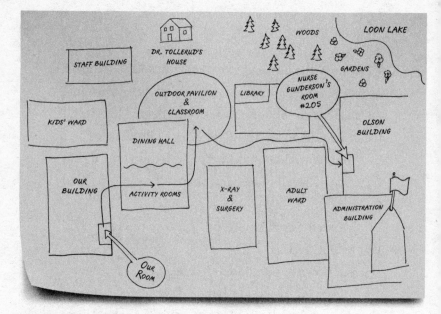

CHAPTER 33

Finding Her

OUR PLAN WAS SIMPLE. We'd skip class—Mr. Blandiss never noticed who was there anyway, since one bundled student looked the same as the next— and go to the Olson Building. Dena had managed to find out Nurse Gunderson's room number from an aide on the children's ward who'd been partial to Dena's brother, Mickey. She'd also drawn me a map with the Olson Building and room 205 marked on it.

But there were loads of ways for this simple plan to go wrong.

Like getting lost.

Or getting found.

Or not getting there at all.

Or not getting back.

But we set out anyway. We headed toward the pavilion. Mr. Blandiss was making his way to his chair, a copy of *Romeo and Juliet* in his gloved hand.

"Look," Dena said, pointing to the number of chairs already filled with people bundled up and ready to listen. "Bet the ladies are hoping to hear him read a love scene!"

I took this as a sign we'd picked the right day. Dena led the way. We stayed outside first, on a short path between buildings. We were counting on blending in with other patients going to class or Activity along the maze of shoveled walkways. With the walls of snow along either side, we wouldn't be taking any shortcuts out here.

We ducked into a building, and Dena pointed to a staircase. "Come on," she said, "let's head to the basement. Fewer people and not so cold."

Big pipes gurgled on the walls alongside us, and the air—too warm and clammy—smelled like the inside of an old woolen mitten.

Up ahead, we heard voices—men's voices. Dena leaned her ear against a closed door and gave the handle a try. With the tilt of her head she signaled me to follow. I scurried into the dark space, trying to sidestep objects. What junk was stored in this room?

The men, only feet away and too busy with their own debate, didn't seem to hear us. "Roosevelt won't be satisfied until we're in there fighting too," one man said. The other disagreed. "FDR doesn't want to go after those blasted Germans again!"

Once their voices and footsteps got swallowed up by the long basement hallway, Dena cracked the door open and made sure no one else was coming. My eyes blinked at the bright light, and Dena had to pull me along, first around a corner, then up a staircase. "This way," she said as we reentered the main floor.

The familiar wheezing and coughing let us know we were back among patients. A nurse headed into one of the rooms; two orderlies pushed wheelchairs down the hall ahead. Dena pointed toward a side door, then with a quick glance to check on me, hurried outside, along a short path and toward a different building.

I trailed behind, struggling to move my slogging feet forward. Did my legs feel this way because of the TB? Was I about to have a hemorrhage? Or was I just tired from walking so much and so fast?

We managed to get through the door and into another stairwell without being caught. We drooped against the wall to rest. "Olson Building," she said between fast breaths.

Moisture trickled down my chest. I hadn't had a feverish sweat like this in months. I tugged at my coat's thick collar and undid the top three buttons.

Then Dena bumped her shoulder against mine and gestured up toward a heavy wooden door with a brass 2 on it to mark the second floor. "There!"

We shoved off from the wall and started climbing.

Just then, someone walked into the stairwell on a floor above us. We stopped moving. The sounds of footsteps clattered and ricocheted off the walls.

But no one appeared. A door upstairs swished opened, then slammed shut, sucking all noise out of the stairwell.

We remained still for another moment, then let our bodies soften back to life. I nudged Dena, but she didn't move. Instead she said, "She could look bad, real bad."

I leaned against the railing, uncertain what to do. Then I saw Dena bow her head and press her mittened hands together. She started to pray, and I did too. After we whispered "Amen" together, we climbed the remaining stairs and turned down a hallway. Side by side, we made our way into Nurse Gunderson's room.

CHAPTER 34

Losing Her

OUR BREATH was taken away by what we saw.

I blinked, hoping each time my eyes opened to find the Nurse Gunderson I remembered.

Instead, she looked like a face in the blurry background of an old photograph, someone hard to recognize. Only her soft blond hair seemed familiar.

She was resting, her skin moonlight pale. Were her eyes still blue? Could the disease wear away their color?

I pulled out the fan from inside my coat. Attached at the base was a thin gold ring with a little tag. Pearl had written on it the words "From your friend Pearl." I could tell by the decorative sweep and fancy curlicues that Pearl must have practiced writing her signature countless times, maybe hoping to be famous someday like one of her movie stars.

On the fan's thin wooden edge I had added the title to Pearl's unfinished poem, "Our Spirits, Too, Will Soar." Dena dug into her pocket to pull out a sheet of stationery on which she'd written, "She would have wanted you to have this." We'd both agreed it was best not to sign the note.

I opened up the fan to see Pegasus one last time. The white horse, his wings spread wide across the delicate paper, seemed about to rise up into a starlit sky. A ray of sunlight from the nearby window beamed through the paper and made the fan's wooden ribs stand out.

Dena gave my arm a gentle tug. I folded the fan closed and wrapped it in the letter. I nestled the slender package under the edge of Nurse Gunderson's pillow and hoped she would find it there.

Perhaps I let the paper crackle too much, or jostled the pillow slightly, because Nurse Gunderson opened her eyes and looked at us.

"Nurse Gunderson," I said, eager to talk to her

even if just for a moment. It didn't seem fair to have come so far and not have the chance to say hello—or maybe good-bye.

Her eyes stared up with a new intensity, as if all the color drained from the rest of her body had now been channeled through them. And yet, despite their blazing blueness, they showed no sign of recognizing us or hearing me, and fluttered closed.

My own eyes blurred with tears. I leaned in toward Nurse Gunderson and spoke in a hurried whisper. "Sarah wishes you well too."

"We have to go," Dena said, turning away.

I rushed along behind Dena—out into the hallway and onto a landing by a window overlooking the snowy paths outdoors. Dena had a new worry in her eyes. "Look! No other patients are out there. We've got to use the tunnels."

The basement had been bad enough. The maze of underground tunnels that connected all the buildings would be even worse.

Dena didn't wait for me to debate the point. I had no choice but to follow her, my tired legs tottering to keep up.

We pushed through a heavy door and into an eerie glow, moving through a jumbled mix of muffled and loud sounds, as if lost in a monster's belly. I caught up to Dena and stayed close.

We edged our way around a corner and could see up ahead an intersection where several tunnels converged. Was one of these the death chute, where, rumor had it, dead bodies got tossed away? Might we hear the rumble of a box going down the long throat of the tunnel? Fear knocked around inside me.

Dena spotted a small sign on one door, read it, then turned herself around as she sorted out exactly where we were. "Not far now," she said just as we heard voices approaching from one of the connecting tunnels.

She pointed to a door on the other side of the brightly lit area ahead of us. "In there!"

I knew we could be crossing right in front of the people in the other tunnel. Would they still be far enough back or perhaps too distracted to notice us?

I had to hope Dena knew what she was doing. And that my legs could move fast. I wasn't sure of either. Suddenly, as if Sarah sensed I needed her, I heard her voice in my head telling me to count to ten fast. Ten steps and we could be through the door.

I grabbed Dena's arm and charged into the light, letting my feet do the math for both of us. Ten steps and we were there—safe!

But we had to rest. I pulled us forward and into a narrow, deep space where a mop and bucket were stored. Scruffy, grainy sounds wheezed up from my lungs; Dena snorted a cough into her coat's heavy sleeve. From our dark cubbyhole, we could hear voices and footsteps but could see no people, as if we were hiding among ghosts.

Finally, Dena tapped my arm and spoke in shorthand. "Now."

I followed her up and out into the icy light on the edge of the pavilion. We merged with others on the paths. We hooked arms and walked in slow, sad steps, as if dragging a wagon heavy with Loon Lake sorrows behind us.

Dear S,

    We saw her, though not certain she saw us. We left her the fan and wished her well.

    Come back soon. Promise.

Love,
E

CHAPTER 35

Good-bye

DENA'S SIXTEENTH birthday was on February 5, and this time I was ready with a gift for her. In my best handwriting, I'd put together a collection of famous poems. I began with her favorite, "Invictus" by William Ernest Henley. I'd read it to her so many times, I could copy it down from memory. I ended with "Tree at My Window" by Robert Frost—the poem I'd given to Sarah for Hanukkah—because Dena had liked his last name. I tied them all together with a piece of yarn from the Activity room.

I'd wanted to give her the present the night before her birthday, but Dena complained of a headache and was asleep before our evening milk arrived. Dena wouldn't want any fuss made anyway.

In the morning, before Nurse Marshall started our routine, she brought in a wheelchair with a large bag resting on it. Dena and I both knew what was happening: she was moving today to the adult ward. She opened her drawer to empty its contents into the bag. She didn't look at me as she transferred her dragon fan, but I knew just by the careful way she handled it what she was feeling. Same with the picture of Mickey.

After breakfast, Dr. Keith examined Dena, making sure she got some aspirin for her headache and letting her know he would still be checking on her in her new ward. I was glad to hear that. Then he helped her into the wheelchair and handed the bag to Nurse Marshall to carry.

I waited, and as they made their way to the door, I got out of bed and placed the poems in Dena's hand. She said nothing and kept her eyes straight ahead. But as she crossed the threshold, she lifted the poems in salute and said, "Just go on, Evvy. Go on."

CHAPTER 36

Letting Go

IN MARCH two new girls joined the room alongside the still-unhappy Janelle. The girls, Vera and Gerty, had just turned twelve and were moved up together from the children's ward. They were thrilled to have each other and remarkably good at tuning Janelle out. Maybe that was easier after living in a ward full of crying children.

I celebrated my fourteenth birthday with a card and a package from home as the only proof that April 9 was different from any other day. Abe had sent me a little pocket dictionary with a smooth leather cover and a red ribbon to mark the pages. I often fell asleep with it in my hand.

Father had tucked an old photo of Abe and me inside a Burpee's seed catalog for spring. Across the cover photo of tulips, he'd written, "With my two lips, I send my love and birthday wishes." In print so tiny I almost missed it at first, he'd written under "Burpee's," "Excuse Mee's!" Mother gave me some stationery with a fancy *E* sweeping across the top.

Grandma had clipped articles, advertisements, and photos—all about the famous Dionne quintuplets. In one picture, the five identical girls were posed with the doctor who had delivered them. Grandma had written on the back of that one—"All doctors good!" As much as Grandma disapproved of the ways people used the quints to make money, she was fascinated by them and assumed because I was a twin I would like reading about them too. I was curious, but not much more than that.

I got to see Dena sometimes in class and heard from her more about the outside world. "They let us read some of the newspapers," Dena explained after she told me that Greece, too, had fallen to Hitler. "I'd enlist if they'd ever let me." Any army would be lucky to get Dena.

Once, I'd asked her about Nurse Gunderson, and Dena just shook her head. "No news."

And then, at the start of May, Mr. Blandiss eloped with one of the patients, both of them leaving Loon Lake AMA—against medical advice—and causing quite a stir. Until they could find a new teacher, our classes were canceled. I didn't miss the schoolwork, but I was sorry not to see Dena either there or at Activity, since she now worked with the grown-ups. She got a note to me once or twice, but then those stopped coming, as did any real mail from Beverly.

I'd watched Dr. Keith more closely ever since the trip to visit Nurse Gunderson back in January. Would I be able to tell in his eyes if she had taken a turn for the worse, or maybe even gotten better? Sometimes I wondered if he'd seen the fan we left. If he had, he never said anything, probably thinking it had been given to her by a patient a long time ago.

In some ways it did feel like a long time ago. With the calendar Grandma had sent me for Christmas I kept better track of the time, but that felt more like a curse than a blessing. It had been seven months since Beverly got discharged, over five since Pearl died and

Sarah got transferred, and three since Dena moved up to the adult ward. Hours and days would go by and I wouldn't think about Nurse Gunderson, at least, not in the way I used to—wanting her back in our room, singing in my ear, and telling us stories about horses or the stars. More and more, I was letting go of life back home too. Now I was the one who had the tall stack of letters tied with a string in my drawer. I always read my mail, but home now felt far away, as if it had been moved to a distant planet where I might not even be able to breathe the strange air.

The only person I held on to tighter than ever was Sarah.

One day, as Dr. Keith checked my pulse, I looked up and just asked, "Is Sarah ever coming back to our room?"

I expected my question to be ignored or, at best, met with a serious look. Instead he answered, "Next week. Her progress has been considerable. You'll be pleased. I intend for you both to continue your steady improvement. Is that understood?"

"Yes," I said, stunned and excited at once.

"Fine, then." He listened to my lungs and finished up the exam as if nothing out of the ordinary had been said.

Sarah's better! She's coming back! These words charmed me more than all the fancy ones I'd been finding in the dictionary Abe sent me.

Then I realized something else: Dr. Keith thought I was getting better too. He had talked about our "steady improvement"—mine as well as Sarah's. Could that really be true? I hadn't had a high fever for a long time and had been gaining weight. I'd noticed that my ankles were sticking out from my pajama pants—maybe I was actually growing again! Sometimes I even felt a rustle of energy inside me and wanted to test my legs like a spring colt eager to run.

Now I just had to prove to myself and to Sarah that we could share a room and still continue to get better. That would be our new promise.

MAY 1941

SUNDAY	MONDAY	TUESDAY	WEDNESDAY	THURSDAY	FRIDAY	SATURDAY
				1	2	3
4	5	6	7	8	9	10
11 MOTHER'S DAY	12	13	14	15	16	17
18	19	20	21	22	23	24
25	26	27	28	29	30 MEMORIAL DAY	31

CHAPTER 37

Bed Post

MISS WANDA wheeled Sarah back into the room May 8, 1941, at 9:27 A.M.

I had just finished my morning glass of buttermilk when I looked up and saw Sarah smiling at me.

Dr. Keith was right. I was pleased. More than pleased. Her face looked softer and fuller and had some color, as if painted in watercolors now instead of etched in charcoal. I watched her step out of the chair and climb into bed on her own. She still looked skinny, but not so bony and frail.

Sarah was sorry she hadn't returned in time to see Dena. And since classes had been canceled, I couldn't share the good news of Sarah's return with

Dena either. We did laugh together over a funny note Dena had sent Sarah shortly after being moved up to the adult building.

Dear Sarah,
  Grown-ups are the biggest crybabies of all.

                              Dena

I knew Dena would be pleased that Sarah and I had made a pact not to talk so much. We'd found a better way to communicate anyway. With the new girls and Janelle in the room with us, we started scribbling notes back and forth instead. That's how I first told Sarah more about seeing Nurse Gunderson.

I couldn't have done it without Dena.

Did you talk to Nurse G?

Not much. She was too sick. I did tell her we all missed her.

Good.

Maybe, but I'm not sure she knew we were even there.

She knew, Evvy. I just know she did.

In her notes to me, Sarah wrote that Dr. Keith had loaned her a book on medicine that he got from the university. She'd discovered she really liked the chapter on vision. She drew me some sketches about how the eyeball works.

Pretty neat!

Pretty scary!

Evvy, I've decided. I want to be ~~an~~ ~~opthomologist~~ ~~an optomologist~~ an eye doctor!

You'll be a great ophthalmologist, Sarah! (Thanks, Abe, for the dictionary.)

I nicknamed our mail system the Bed Post. Our messages eventually got tossed into the brown bags with our soiled tissues, so we didn't worry too much that Nurse Marshall or anyone else would bother to read them. Over time, we started to write about more private matters.

Sarah told me more about being Jewish, including how she'd once been jeered by other children at Easter for "killing Jesus." I'd almost written "Didn't they know

Jesus was Jewish?" then remembered I hadn't known that fact either until Sarah had told me. So instead I wrote "I'm sorry that happened." Those few words hardly seemed enough. I wished I could have borrowed Abe's blue crayon to show her how I really felt.

But we also wrote back and forth about more lighthearted things. One day Sarah told me she spoke some Yiddish. I didn't know what Yiddish was but figured if it was a language, people in some country must speak it.

Where's Yiddy, Sarah?

It's not a country, Evvy, just a language. Jewish people speak it.

Is there a Jewish country?

Not yet. Maybe someday. My father hopes for that.

So where did Yiddish come from?

Who knows? Father says it's like German. But it's got some Hebrew and French and Russian in it too.

Sounds like a real mishmash to me.

Evvy!!! You speak Yiddish. "Mishmash" is a Yiddish word!

Pretty funny! Hey, I can teach you some German words, Sarah.

Like what?

"Kaffeeklatsch"—Grandma used to say that when the ladies got together to share gossip over coffee.

I get it. "Kaffee" must be coffee.

Right. But Grandma tried to stop using German words a while ago. I guess it's not a good time to be German either.

With Sarah back, the May anniversary of my arrival at Loon Lake seemed bearable. Our flurry of Bed Post notes had me laughing instead of crying about those first miserable weeks here.

Maybe because Sarah and I had been separated for so many months and could only imagine talking or writing to each other all that time, our system of sending notes back and forth suited us. I liked it best when I made Sarah giggle; she liked it best when she made me think. And we both liked feeling we were getting better—together, one Loon Lake day at a time.

CHAPTER 38

Midnight Journey

"EVVY, WAKE UP," a voice said.

A male voice. Familiar but somehow not familiar too. Not Abe's or my father's—even in my groggy state I knew that.

"What?" I lifted my head off the pillow.

"Don't be alarmed," the voice said in such a reassuring way I almost drifted back to sleep.

"Do you think you could walk a ways, Evvy?" the voice asked.

The voice—it was Dr. Keith speaking. As my eyes adjusted, I made out his silhouette—his slumped shoulders, his scribbled hair, his wire eyeglasses.

"I shouldn't ask this of anyone," he mumbled.

"Ask what, Dr. Keith?" I looked around to be certain he wasn't talking to someone else. "Do you need my help?"

"Yes, Evvy, I do," he said. "Or more important, she does."

A wave of worry washed over me.

He leaned over my bed. "Can you get yourself up and into your robe and shoes? I need you to come with me. Now."

"Okay," I whispered, and slid my feet out of bed.

"I'm coming too!" Sarah called out from the dark.

Dr. Keith spun on his heel to face Sarah's bed. "No, Sarah."

But she insisted. "I'll go in a wheelchair, and Evvy can walk."

Dr. Keith took off his glasses and rubbed his eyes. "I really shouldn't have come at all."

"But you did," Sarah said, "and we're going to help. Just like Evvy helped me."

Sarah's determination fueled m[...]
together, Dr. Keith, or not at all."

He turned away, his shoes scuffin[...]
floor.

I couldn't blame him for leaving. We'd j[...]
plicated whatever plan he had. Still, I was [...]
pointed and tried halfheartedly to convince m[...]
that seeing Nurse Gunderson might not be the b[...]
idea—for Sarah or for me.

Then I heard a whir, whir, whir and footsteps.
Dr. Keith was back, pushing a wheelchair to Sarah's
bed.

"She needs you," he said, as if that explained
everything. "Just don't wake the others."

I put on my robe, then grabbed Sarah's and let
Dr. Keith help her into the wheelchair. I made my
way to the little closet where Up Patients stored
their additional clothes and slipped on my shoes.
Then I waited in the blurry darkness for Dr. Keith
and Sarah.

Sarah whispered, "I need to go to the bathroom."

"Can you help her, Evvy?" Dr. Keith didn't wait
for a response. "I'll wait here."

At night, a soft light was left on in the bathroom,
making it easier for me to guide Sarah where she
needed to be. I had never helped anyone use a toilet

)efore. I faced Sarah, put my arms under hers, and eased her up. She tipped a bit as she pulled down her pajama pants, but I didn't let her fall. I had to squat down in front of her, face-to-face, and keep my arms on either side so she didn't lose her balance. I could feel the indentation where Sarah's rib had been taken out—and hoped my pressing arm didn't hurt her. For a moment, nothing happened. I crossed my eyes and made a funny face, and we both giggled. Sarah finished, and I helped her back into the wheelchair, to the sink to wash her hands, then out the door.

Dr. Keith guided us with urgent, quick steps down our familiar hallway to another and then to another not familiar at all.

The sanatorium looked so different late at night. Had I ever used this corridor to go out to the pavilion? Wasn't the stairwell on the right instead of the left? Were there always chairs in that alcove?

In a matter of minutes, I felt as confused as I had my first day at Loon Lake.

A nurse passed by and bowed her head slightly. "Good evening, Dr. Keith." Her eyes glided over Sarah and me as if we were invisible.

He then led us into an area that must have been used for visitors, since we heard no coughing and saw neither patients nor staff. I knew Dena and I had

never come through here, though maybe by this point she and I had gone into the tunnels or were skirting along the outside wall. I wished Dena were with us now, but I couldn't complicate Dr. Keith's plan further by asking to go get her.

We stepped out of the building into the cool night air. The stars pulsed overhead, as if to signal we were getting closer to Nurse Gunderson.

Once in the next building, we faced the elevators. "I know what this will mean to her," said Dr. Keith as he pushed the button once, then again, then a third time. At last an elevator arrived. Dr. Keith swung Sarah's chair around and backed into the small space. Then I hurried to step in alongside before the big doors closed. All three of us looked up at the line of numbers, staring at the yellowish 1 as if our concentration alone could lift the elevator off the ground.

After a long second, the machinery clunked, then surged, and the elevator began going up. We whirred past the second floor. Isn't that where Nurse Gunderson had been? I was sure of that, but maybe she'd been moved.

The elevator hummed as it slowed to stop at the third floor. The doors opened onto a busy hall. Nurses scurried about, seeming to go in all directions at once. I gave Sarah a perplexed look. This seemed so different from the quiet floor where Nurse Gunderson had been before.

Dr. Keith forged ahead through a door and into a place unlike any other I'd seen at Loon Lake. This room was long and narrow, with a single line of beds stretching to both our left and right. Ahead of us was a wall of blackness. Not a wall, I realized, but a series of floor-to-ceiling windows running the length of the room. All the beds faced these opened windows, but there was no breeze; the place still had the musty, sour smell of a forgotten corner in a basement.

Why had Dr. Keith allowed Nurse Gunderson to be here? Was she being punished because they loved each other?

Dr. Keith turned left down the aisle that ran between the beds and the windows. I couldn't stop myself from looking at one patient after the next—grown women looking as feeble as babies, some even crying. I wouldn't have lasted a day here. How could Nurse Gunderson stand it?

I reached for Sarah as Dr. Keith guided us the last steps.

And so together, hand in hand, Sarah and I saw her resting like a frail leaf atop the last bed by the wall.

It wasn't Nurse Gunderson.

It was Dena.

Our Dena.

"She's been drifting in and out of a coma," Dr. Keith said, checking her pulse. "I thought maybe seeing you . . ." He gave up explaining and stepped back against the wall.

Sarah pulled her wheelchair in closer as I sank onto the bed. Someone had pushed back the damp strands of Dena's dark hair, which made her face seem small and naked.

"Dena, it's us, Evvy and Sarah," I whispered.

Her eyes moved under her half-closed lids. Did she know us? Could she tell we were here? Could she feel our hands holding hers?

"Dena," I said again, leaning in close enough to hear her shallow, fast breaths and to feel the fever rising hot from her skin.

"Tell her a poem," Sarah said.

I knew which poem Dena would want to hear. I just didn't know if I could bear to say it.

Then I closed my eyes and began reciting her favorite poem.

INVICTUS
by William Ernest Henley

Out of the night that covers me,
Black as the pit from pole to pole,
I thank whatever gods may be
For my unconquerable soul.

In the fell clutch of circumstance
I have not winced nor cried aloud.
Under the bludgeonings of chance
My head is bloody, but unbowed.

Beyond this place of wrath and tears
Looms but the horror of the shade,
And yet the menace of the years
Finds and shall find me unafraid.

It matters not how strait the gate,
How charged with punishments the scroll,
I am the master of my fate;
I am the captain of my soul.

My eyes opened as I said the last lines, hoping to find Dena awake, ready to bark at me about sneaking off again.

But she remained pale and still.

The night sounds of coughs and cries circled around us, but we listened only for the silence.

Then it came. Dena had gone home.

June 26, 1941

Dear Abe,

It took more than a year, but I've finally seen the lake and a loon. Sarah was with me, since Dr. Keith lets me wheel her outside now.

I'm sorry you won't ever get to meet Dena. What happened has been hard on everybody. Especially Dr. Keith. He hasn't gotten in trouble like I worried about. No one's said anything to Dr. Tollerud. I figure everyone here would just as soon die holding the hand of a friend, so they want to stay on Dr. Keith's good side.

I'm just not sure Dr. Keith believes he did the right thing taking us to her. He knew Dena's TB had gone into her brain when she started having bad headaches. There was nothing more he

→

could do except give her comfort. But he didn't mean for us to see her die.

I tried to tell him it would have been worse if Dena had been alone. We got to hold her hand and know she's in a safe place with her brother. I'd settle for that.

As for the lake, it's not all that big and by Minnesota standards not all that pretty. But sometimes just being alive makes everything look good.

Love,
Evvy

CHAPTER 39

A Different Path

"LET'S WALK HERE today, Sarah, instead of going
to the concert." I guided the wheelchair down a
paved path that wandered alongside a wooded area
and away from the other patients.

In the weeks since Dena's death, Sarah and I
had spent as much time as we could outdoors, as if
the summer sun could ease the memory of that
dark night.

Sarah looked over her shoulder. "You're thinking
about Dena, aren't you?"

I looked away to avoid meeting Sarah's eyes. I
was thinking about Dena, but about something
else too. About what Dr. Keith had told me after
my last X-ray.

"I was wondering," I said, remembering something else, "if we should send a letter to tell Beverly—like we did after Pearl."

"We'll do it later today, Evvy. I've got that new stationery my mother sent. We'll tell Beverly you're getting better too."

Does Sarah already know? No, she couldn't. Dr. Keith had made a point of talking to me privately in an examination room, away from Sarah and the other girls.

I kept pushing the wheelchair, glad the path moved from the shade of the woods into the warm sunshine of a green lawn. "I'm not the only one getting better, Sarah. You can write that in the letter too."

Sarah pointed to the grassy side of the path. "Let's go sit over there."

I hesitated an instant. Face-to-face, I knew I wouldn't be able to keep anything from Sarah. I slowed down and eased the wheelchair to a stop, then spread out a small blanket. With my help, Sarah soon rested comfortably on the ground. I sat beside her and braided stems of clover into a long chain.

She turned her face to the sun and closed her eyes. "You know, Evvy, now that you're leaving Loon Lake, I promise to be okay even without you here."

The clover necklace dropped from my hands. "Sarah, how did you— I mean, when did you—"

She'd solved yet another mystery.

Sarah opened her eyes and smiled at me. "I've been seeing it coming for a while, Evvy. You look healthier than most of the staff these days. Then this morning, when you came back to the room, you looked like you'd been crying. I figured there was only one thing that could make you cry like that"— she paused and took a deep, clear breath—"knowing you were going to see Abe soon."

I felt a wave of tears rising inside me. "Nope, Sarah," I said. "For once, you're wrong." I lifted my clover chain and placed it on her head like a summer crown. "It was knowing I'd have to say good-bye to you."

I know you'll write me from home, but
will you share your poems with me too?
I hope so. Miss you already . . .

Sarah

CHAPTER 40

Last Night
(July 8, 1941)

DURING MY LAST NIGHT at Loon Lake, I broke its biggest rule: I didn't rest, or at least not much. At first I thought about the Bed Post Sarah had tossed me.

I hadn't written a poem about our friendship. Not yet. I had started lots of times but hadn't finished any, though I had been working hard on one piece. Had Sarah known? Is that why she asked?

Then, as if one worrisome thought nudged another loose, an alarm went off inside me.

I was leaving Sarah.

Leaving her.

Alone.

And maybe forever.

Yes, she was doing better. To reassure myself, I listened to her steady breaths. The scratchy sounds that used to remind me of static on a distant radio station were almost gone now.

But we'd thought Pearl was getting better, and Dena too. If something terrible happened to Sarah, I wouldn't be here even to hold her hand. How could I leave?

But how could I stay? I sat up in bed and hugged my legs close, letting tears dampen the knees of my pajamas. Father was coming to get me. I was going home. This was what I'd been hoping for ever since my first awful night at Loon Lake. I knew Sarah understood that, even if she felt jealous or scared about being left behind. If Sarah had been the first to go home, I would have been happy for her. Plus, she'd been strong enough to handle being alone before. She would tell me she could do it again, and she knew more than anyone else how much I wanted to see Abe. So how could I stay?

My thoughts tumbled and turned. I knew I had to do something. I rummaged through a bag that now held all the things from my drawer. I found what I wanted, then set to work, glad for the light of a full moon.

When I finished, I must have dozed off. I woke to the sounds of the sanatorium coughing back into motion like an old engine starting up. Sarah was already awake. Our morning smiles were interrupted by an orderly wheeling a chair into our room with a blue dress folded over its back and a pair of slip-on shoes on the seat. Nurse Marshall came in and told me to put on the clothes, then went about her morning task of taking temperatures.

I changed in the bathroom, wondering if Nurse Marshall might give Sarah and me a chance to say our good-byes. But if not, Sarah would find what I'd left and understand.

The dress buttoned up the front and fitted at my waist with a matching belt. I brushed my hair and put on the shoes, then I glanced in the mirror. I looked healthier already just being out of hospital clothes, but stranger too. I stepped back into the room, feeling out of place now with the others.

Dr. Keith was there, standing by the wheelchair and waiting for me. I hurried to sit down, embarrassed by the carefree swoosh of the dress. Then I noticed a second wheelchair. He took it to Sarah's bed and helped her into it, then wheeled us one at a time out the door and to a corner at the end of the hall.

"I can only give you a moment alone together," he said, lining us up side by side. Then he leaned in toward us, his stethoscope falling forward like a floppy necktie, and said in a quieter tone, "I've also been instructed by a certain nurse, who is doing better, to tell you she's your fan too." He straightened back up, smiled at us both, and then was off.

"Do you think he knows?" I asked.

"You mean, about you and Dena sneaking in to see Nurse Gunderson?" Sarah said, then answered with a laugh. "Of course he does, Ev!" She reached over and squeezed my arm. "Where do you think he got the idea for taking us to see Dena?"

I nodded, afraid if I tried to speak right now, tears would follow.

"I'm glad we were there," Sarah said, still holding my arm. "Together."

"Me too," I whispered, then took a deep breath, as if to clear the way for the words still inside me. "Listen, Sarah, I finished a poem and left it in your drawer. I wrote it about Dena. But it's really for you—for us—about going on. Like Dena told me."

"Then let's promise to do that, Ev."

Nurse Marshall made her way down the hallway toward us.

"Here comes Old Eagle Eye," I said, putting my hand on Sarah's, wishing I wouldn't have to let go.

Sarah lowered her voice. "You'd better not write me that you're missing her!"

Before I could answer, Nurse Marshall was there and wheeling her away.

Sarah turned her head and looked back at me with a smile. I waved good-bye with a hand still warm from holding hers.

To Dena,
who was the captain of her soul

Morning
by Evelyn Hoffmeister

The cold night blows a lonely dust
And scatters hope and faith and trust.
I mourn that I must learn to mourn
To find the whole in what's been torn.
But still I do not welcome death,
I welcome life, each morning's breath.

CHAPTER 41

Going Home

I SAT IN A WHEELCHAIR and waited for Father to arrive. Would he be alone? Would the whole family come?

I thought about what Dr. Keith had told me yesterday morning. How my guinea pig had lived—a sign that my body had built walls around the disease in my lungs. How my sputum had been clear of tuberculosis for months. How my lungs looked and sounded good and how I'd gained weight and strength. And how, as long as I took care of myself and let those walls stand, I could lead a full life.

Nurse Marshall had still worn a mask over her mouth when she wheeled me to the visitor's lobby: I would never be cured in her eyes. She'd left a large bag by my side and said "Good luck" in such an awkward way that she'd made me feel like my chances of even making it out the door were slim.

I held the other, smaller bag on my lap with my letters and things from my bedside table. When I'd emptied the drawer, I'd found something else—Dena's envelope stuffed with the bottle caps from our cola party. She must have put it in my drawer before she'd left our room. I didn't say anything to Sarah. Instead, in the night, I tucked it deep into her drawer to find, maybe on the day she was discharged too.

Now, with no sign of Father, I reached down into the larger bag to make sure my belongings were all there, especially my green book of poems from Mother and the little dictionary from Abe. My fingers instead bumped into something cushiony soft and familiar. Francy, my stuffed bear! Nurse Marshall hadn't thrown her away after all. I started to lift her out, but decided to wait until later. I wanted Father to see how much I'd grown up.

I looked out the window again, this time at the flowerbeds full of pink and white and red petunias lining the long drive. Then, off in the distance, I saw a Lincoln Zephyr making its way up the road and toward the building.

"He's here," I said, bouncing up in my seat,

though no one heard or seemed interested in my announcement.

"He's here," I said again, this time just for myself.

I stood and held my bags, then took slow steps—careful not to attract attention by running—to the giant door.

I walked into the bright sunshine and started down the stairs on my own.

Father was waving his handkerchief from his car window to greet me.

Before the car even came to a full stop, a back door winged open and someone flew out and up the steps to me. Someone so tall I almost called him Father, but instead I cried out, "Abe!"

CHAPTER 42

Blank Pages

MOTHER AND I had the house to ourselves—the first time since I'd returned a week ago. Father and Abe had driven Grandma Hoffmeister back home, agreeing to repair her wobbly porch railing in exchange for a dinner of ribs and sauerkraut. I rested, my cheek pressed against an old lace doily on the sofa's arm, while Mother worked.

"Sometimes at Loon Lake I pretended you were singing to me," I told her as she sorted through stacks of music in preparation for her new job as choir director at our church.

She looked up. "Any piece in particular?"

"You know those poems Father used to read to us from *A Child's Garden of Verses*—the song versions?"

"Mmm," she said, her voice holding the note in her musical way. "I'm pleased you remember."

"I do. I told the girls how you'd sing to us and how Father used to threaten Abe and me that if we didn't sit still, he'd plant us in some dirt to see if we'd grow a verse or two."

Mother arched an eyebrow and laughed. "Yes, I do seem to recall your father saying something along those lines."

"Did you know that Robert Louis Stevenson also had tuberculosis?" I asked.

She bent down to check for something in a box of music on the floor and didn't seem to hear me. Or maybe she just didn't want me ever to say that dreaded word again.

"Stevenson wrote *A Child's Garden of Verses*," I reminded her.

She walked over to the piano and thumbed through some music. "Like the one you always liked best, 'The Land of Counterpane'?" She flattened the music open with the palm of her hand, then played and sang along.

Her hands seemed to float across the piano, as if she didn't actually have to touch the keys, only signal them with her fingertips, the music happening by magic. As she sang her face softened, turning the words into a lullaby until a happy sleepiness came over me.

The music ended, and I opened my eyes. Had I drifted off for a moment? I must have, because Mother had gone back to sorting her music again.

"One of his poems was in the book you sent me," I told her in a dreamy sort of way, aware that a light blanket now covered me and felt good tucked around my shoulders. "I read that book over and over—"

"Oh, you just reminded me," Mother said, putting her finger to her lips as if to think for a moment, then leaving the room. I could hear her heels click up the stairs, then across the floor in the bedroom.

I closed my eyes and listened to the sounds outside the open window.

I heard cats—maybe Sweetie or one of her grown kittens—hissing and quarreling. I listened to a truck off in the distance as it slowed down to turn a corner, something clanging and clunking against the walls of the truck's bed. I thought of the metal carts rattling down the hallway at Loon Lake.

Over everything else, I heard the zeet-zeet-zeet of the crickets. Once I started paying attention, that noise seemed as relentless as all the coughing at Loon Lake. I wished I could tell Mother about nights there and about Sarah and Dena—the other girls too—and Nurse Gunderson and Dr. Keith.

But some part of me realized that what happened at Loon Lake would always be background noise for her. She could not hear it as music, and I could not sing it to her.

"I got this for you," she said, coming back into the room and walking to the sofa. In her outstretched hand was a present. I sat up, the blanket tumbling off me. She handed me the gift, then, with the elegant poise of someone about to face an audience, seated herself in a nearby chair.

She waved her hand toward the package, conducting me to open it.

My fingers tugged at the ribbons and wrapping. I could feel that a book rested inside, and I glanced up, wanting again to say how much I'd loved the other book she'd given me, how much those poems had meant to us all.

But Mother looked down at the gift—eager or impatient, I couldn't quite tell—so I hurried to reveal this book's cover.

When I did, I was surprised to see that nothing was written across the red leather on the front or on its binding either. Inside, there were no words: the pages were as white as the walls at Loon Lake.

This was not a regular book, it was a journal.

The cover felt buttery soft in my hands, and already ideas were coming to me about what I would include in the book—maybe a poem about Sarah, and, oh, a dedication, and I'd have to decide how I wanted to sign my name. . . .

I looked up and smiled. "Thank you," I said, and squeezed my journal as if it were her hand. "It's perfect."

"You're welcome, Evvy." She stood to return to her work, then paused and said, "I could tell from your letters that you're a writer."

"I'm a writer," I whispered, as if repeating a refrain—maybe from one of her songs or from one of my poems.

I smiled, knowing we each had our own way—and we both had each other.

I fluttered the blank pages of my journal between my fingers. Little puffs of air blew against my cheek, as if my soon-to-be-written words had already taken their first breath.

AUTHOR'S NOTE

Evidence of tuberculosis has been found in Egyptian mummies; its symptoms are described in ancient Greek and Hindu texts as well as in the Bible. For centuries, people called it "consumption" because of the way the disease seemed to consume the body. After 1882, when Robert Koch discovered the germ that causes the disease and named it the tubercle bacillus, the illness became known as tuberculosis.

Tuberculosis is a contagious disease, spread most commonly by coughing. Fortunately, most people who are exposed to the germ never actually become ill. But many people do, and up until the mid-1940s, there was little effective treatment. At that time, armed with a new drug called streptomycin, doctors at the Mayo Clinic in Rochester, Minnesota, successfully treated a woman who would have otherwise died of the disease. She recovered and went on to lead a full and active life. In the years following, doctors found that with the right combination of medicines, patients could be treated successfully. Many thought the White Plague—as tuberculosis was sometimes called—had been conquered. In recent years, however, new strains have proven resistant to these drugs, and an estimated two million people still die of tuberculosis worldwide each year.

Different types of tuberculosis can affect all parts of the body, including the bones, skin, throat, brain, and internal organs. In *Breathing Room*, the girls have pulmonary tuberculosis, the most common form affecting the lungs. If the body cannot resist the invading bacteria, the healthy tissue in the lungs dies and dissolves away, leaving behind a cavity. Dead tissue and the active bacteria get coughed up in sputum, a mix of saliva and mucous. Eventually more and more of these cavities form until, in some cases, the inside of the lung is dotted with holes, like a slice of Swiss cheese. Over time, the erosive process may also damage a large blood vessel. When this happens, the blood vessel can rupture and the patient experiences excessive bleeding, called a hemorrhage. Because the blood is fresh with oxygen from the lungs, it is bright red and foamy from the coughing. Some patients die from a hemorrhage, while others recover over time.

Tuberculosis affects each patient differently, though common symptoms include fever, exhaustion, vomiting, weight loss, rapid heartbeat, and—most notably—a lingering bad cough. But there is no set course for the disease. In one patient, the illness remains in check and causes little damage. Some patients don't even know they have tuberculosis—the illness is not discovered until an autopsy. (This was the case with First Lady Eleanor Roosevelt; after her death, an autopsy revealed she had died of tuberculosis.) In another patient, the disease overwhelms the body so quickly that the patient dies within weeks or months of the diagnosis.

In the past, the unpredictable nature of the disease made it hard for doctors to evaluate various treatments. For example, an operation might bring about a recovery for one patient, but the same procedure in a different patient might have no effect or even cause harm. Was the operation a success or a failure? Chances are, neither. The disease was just following its own course, independent of the operation or the doctor's care. In *Breathing Room*, Dena and Sarah both receive a popular treatment of the time— the pneumothorax, called a "pneumo" by the patients. The goal was to blow air into the chest in order to flatten the lung and give it a rest. In the story Sarah also weathers a thoracoplasty, an operation in which ribs were removed to allow the lung to collapse and rest. In other operations, nerves to the chest area were cut and, in extreme cases, part or all of a lung might be removed. By today's medical standards, many of these operations would be considered questionable since no scientific evidence justifies their risks—everything from disfigurement to blindness to death.

But before antibiotics were available, patients with tuberculosis had few choices. A diagnosis was a virtual death sentence, made worse by the knowledge that the patient was contagious. Then, in the late 1800s, several doctors made the observation that patients seemed to get better after spending time outside, usually in a cold climate. Almost overnight, special centers called sanatoriums opened all over the world to isolate and treat people suffering from tuberculosis. In the United States, Dr. Edward Livingston Trudeau—himself a sufferer of the disease—established the country's most famous sanatorium at Saranac Lake in the Adirondack Mountains of New York. Other private and public sanatoriums of all sorts and philosophies dotted the country to meet the needs of so many sick people.

Patients "chased the cure" and flocked to these sanatoriums to spend winters outside in cure chairs—now commonly called Adirondack chairs—with the hopes of getting better. Some of these facilities were built with long outdoor porches, called verandas, where patients rested in beds. Most of the patients' rooms had large windows, kept open even in the coldest of weather. Many sanatoriums, like the one imagined in *Breathing Room*, were large complexes, often built in a remote and beautiful setting. Some had their own dairies or small farms to provide fresh milk and vegetables for the patients. Other sanatoriums were smaller, run more like a boarding house than a medical facility.

The one thing all sanatoriums had in common was the absolute conviction that rest was the key to the cure. Patients were ordered to remain in bed on their backs for months or years. Stories of patients living as long as twenty years on bed rest were not uncommon. Eventually if the patient improved, some activity would be allowed, but usually under strict medical supervision.

Doctors and staff took the business of resting very seriously, perhaps too much so. In the majority of first-hand accounts by former patients, doctors and nurses are remembered as cold, controlling, and unsympathetic. Certainly there were exceptions, chief among them Dr. Trudeau, but doctors and nurses (often former TB patients themselves) were not generally described with great affection. According to Dr. Frank Ryan in his book *The Forgotten Plague*, one doctor in Scotland was known for saying of his young female patients: "Here you are, a collection of rosy apples, all rotten at the core." I adapted this line for my novel as a way of showing the cruelty some in authority displayed for those suffering from the disease. Fortunately, not all the sanatorium staff adopted such a negative, heartless attitude. But even the best medical care could not relieve the patients' relentless boredom: endless days with nothing to do other than lie there. Sanatorium gossip, the occasional visitor (some sanatoriums were stricter about visits than others), a special event such as a concert or movie, or the disheartening news of a fellow patient taking a sudden turn for the worse might be the only events to break up the monotony of the daily routine.

Though no accurate statistics about the survival rate of sanatorium patients are available, some think that as many as one in four patients died and as many as half the patients died within five years of leaving the facility. In fact, evidence suggests that the patients in sanatorium care had no greater a survival rate than those who remained at home. But because contagious patients were isolated, the sanatorium movement probably did reduce the spread of the disease in the general population. And since tuberculosis often struck those already weakened by hunger or poor living conditions, sanatoriums—with their emphasis on cleanliness and a high-calorie diet— might have given some patients a better chance for recovery. But in the end, most of the strict rules the girls in *Breathing Room* had to follow probably made little difference in the outcome of their diseases.

In writing *Breathing Room*, I chose to include several references to author Robert Louis Stevenson and his poems. Stevenson himself suffered from tuberculosis and received treatment at Saranac Lake in the Adirondacks, though he eventually died from the disease. But two interesting coincidences involving other famous people cropped up as I worked on the novel. I wanted the character of Dena to take a liking to poetry and to have a favorite poem. But which poem? In searching through a 1938 poetry anthology (actually owned by my mother when she was in high school), I found a poem called "Invictus" by William Ernest Henley that conveyed Dena's thoughts and determination. Only later did I find out that William

Ernest Henley also suffered from tuberculosis. In fact, he wrote "Invictus" as he fought to keep the doctors from amputating his leg. (He had already lost part of his other leg to the disease.) I was surprised to learn that Henley was a close friend of Robert Louis Stevenson's and, with his red hair and partially amputated leg, Henley served as the inspiration for one of Stevenson's most memorable characters, Long John Silver in *Treasure Island*.

I also chose to include in *Breathing Room* talk about the most popular film of the day, *Gone with the Wind*. Only after I finished writing the book did I learn that the actress Vivien Leigh, who played the role of Scarlett O'Hara, suffered from pulmonary tuberculosis for years and, like one of my novel's characters, died from complications following a lung hemorrhage.

On a more personal note, I had several reasons for writing a book about tuberculosis. First, though I never had active tuberculosis or was ill with the disease, I had to take a year of medicine as a preventive treatment after a tuberculin skin test turned up positive. Had I lived forty or fifty years earlier and gotten sick, I might well have found myself at a sanatorium. Secondly, I grew up in Rochester, Minnesota, where my father was a pediatrician at the Mayo Clinic and where, in 1944 to 1945, Dr. Corwin Hinshaw first treated TB patients effectively with the drug streptomycin. Dr. Hinshaw later went on to win the Nobel Prize in Medicine for his work. Though I never knew Dr. Hinshaw, the surgeon who supervised the care of the first patient treated with this new drug was my neighbor, Dr. O. T. "Jim" Clagett. Also, Dr. Alfred G. Karlson, the father of my best friend from childhood, was a microbiologist who studied tuberculosis and did important work on streptomycin and the other drugs that proved effective in combating the disease.

Finally, as a child I was a great fan of Betty MacDonald's books, especially *Nancy and Plum* and the Mrs. Piggle-Wiggle series. Later, as an adult, I discovered her book *The Plague and I*, her account of her time in a sanatorium. That book inspired me to learn more about tuberculosis and to imagine the challenges of sanatorium life for a young person. I found out that in Minnesota alone, every county had a sanatorium. Yet once tuberculosis could be treated, and in many cases cured, with antibiotics, the sanatoriums quickly closed in the 1950s and the stories of all those Evelyns, Sarahs, Denas, Beverlys, and Pearls were lost. Perhaps no one wanted to look back on such a sad time. Or, more likely, once the Japanese bombed Pearl Harbor on December 7, 1941 (just months after the close of the novel), the nation focused its energies on winning the Second World War. In writing this book, I hoped to give those forgotten girls a chance to breathe again.

NOTES ON THE IMAGES

FRONTISPIECE

As part of President Franklin Delano Roosevelt's New Deal program, the Works Progress
Administration (WPA) created this poster to
encourage the public to eat healthy foods as a
way to fight tuberculosis.

CHAPTER 2

The Rochester State Hospital in
Rochester, Minnesota, the author's
hometown. The structure no longer
stands. [History Center of Olmsted
County, Minnesota]

CHAPTER 4

X-rays were used both to diagnose tuberculosis and to monitor the progress of the disease. This is an X-ray viewing room at the Triboro Hospital for Tuberculosis on Parsons Boulevard in Jamaica,

New York. [Library of Congress, Prints and Photographs Division, Gottscho-Schleisner Collection, LC-G612-T-39094]

CHAPTER 5

A standard bedpan of the day, photographed at the Mayo Clinic Historical Unit, Rochester, Minnesota.

CHAPTER 6

Sputum cups—disposable ones that were burned or reusable ones that needed to be disinfected—were used daily at sanatoriums to collect patients' phlegm. Outside the sanatorium, nearly every community had some kind of law and a hefty fine for spitting in public to prevent the spread of tuberculosis.

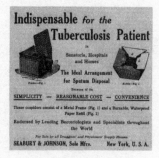

This advertisement was taken from *Journal of the Outdoor Life*, a magazine for patients seeking the cure in Saranac Lake, New York, the home of America's sanatorium movement. [*Journal of the Outdoor Life* (March 1933), courtesy of the Trudeau Institute, Saranac Lake, New York]

CHAPTER 7

Cod-liver oil, a rich source of vitamin D, was often given to children despite its strong fishy flavor. [Courtesy of the Lung Association of Saskatchewan]

"Bottled"   Sunlight"

Extra rich in "sunshine vitamin" D. Possesses a fine, wholesome flavour.

CHAPTER 8

After completing my novel, I found this photograph, taken in 1941, of a ward room at the Triboro Hospital for Tuberculosis in Jamaica, New York. This is exactly how I imagined the room where Evvy and the other girls lived. [Library of Congress, Prints and Photographs Division, Gottscho-Schleisner Collection, LC-G612-T-39046]

CHAPTER 9

Patients' temperatures were taken at least twice daily to monitor their condition. To get an accurate temperature,

A New B-D Fever Thermometer

"MEDICAL CENTER"

Genuine When Marked B-D

A Reliable Thermometer for $1.00 with Case

Sold Through Dealers

BECTON, DICKINSON & CO.   RUTHERFORD, N. J.

the thermometer would need to be in the patient's mouth for at least five minutes, sometimes longer. [*Journal of the Outdoor Life* (March 1933), courtesy of the Trudeau Institute, Saranac Lake, New York]

CHAPTER 11

The headline from a June 14, 1940, Minnesota newspaper. [Courtesy of Library of Congress, permission from the Minneapolis *Star Tribune*]

CHAPTER 11

A poster created by the National Tuberculosis Association (now the American Lung Association) to  promote sales of its Christmas Seals, which served as a source of money to fight tuberculosis. [National Tuberculosis Association posters used with permission © 2011 American Lung Association. www.LungUSA.org]

CHAPTER 12

A U.S. postage stamp commemorating the 1939 World's Fair held in Queens, New York.

CHAPTER 13

Louis Armstrong, one of the most important jazz musicians of the twentieth century, was famous for his dazzling trumpet playing and his distinctive, gravelly singing voice. [William P. Gottlieb Collection, Music Division, Library of Congress, with appreciation to the Louis Armstrong Educational Foundation, Inc.]

CHAPTER 14

A hospital gurney (a stretcher on wheels) transported patients not able to sit upright in a wheelchair. [Courtesy of Urban Remains LLC]

CHAPTER 15

Fluoroscopy allows moving X-ray pictures to be taken of a patient's lungs. [Library of Congress, Prints and Photographs Division, Gottscho-Schleisner Collection, LC-G612-T-39097]

CHAPTER 17

The author grew up in Rochester, Minnesota, home of the world-famous Mayo Clinic, and recalls seeing signs like this one posted on streets around local hospitals. [Used with permission of the Mayo Foundation for Medical Education and Research, all rights reserved.]

CHAPTER 21

This drawing shows the two bottles used during a pneumothorax procedure. Pressure from the water in the elevated bottle pushes air from the lower bottle through the tubing connected to a needle. By measuring the drop in the fluid, the doctor would know how much air had been injected into the patient. [Courtesy of the Lung Association of Saskatchewan]

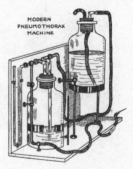

CHAPTER 21

A doctor and nurse perform a pneumothorax on a patient suffering from tuberculosis. The doctor would insert a needle into the small space between the patient's lungs and rib cage, then pump in air. The air from the machine pushed the infected lung down, making it flat. (In a similar— and even stranger—procedure, some doctors surgically inserted Ping-Pong balls into the small space to keep the lung down.)

Without air moving in and out of the lung, the bacteria's growth was hampered. But the procedure needed to be repeated routinely because over time the air would leak out of the space and into the rest of the body. Although pneumothorax procedures were commonly done at sanatoriums, they came with serious risks, including the danger of pushing air into a blood vessel and causing a stroke—or possibly death. [Courtesy of the Lung Association of Saskatchewan]

CHAPTER 22
Hot water bottles—nicknamed "pigs" because old-fashioned ones made of earthenware looked like pigs—were eventually made of heavy rubber and filled with hot water to provide warmth to bedridden patients.

CHAPTER 27
St. Paul Winter Carnival, a Minnesota tradition since the 1880s.

CHAPTER 28

Christmas Seals sold by the Tuberculosis Association raised money for the research and treatment of the disease. [National Tuberculosis Association posters used with permission © 2011 American Lung Association. www.LungUSA.org]

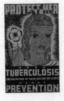

CHAPTER 30

A WPA poster reminds people of the dangers of tuberculosis.

CHAPTER 31

A poetry anthology used by the author's mother in high school during the 1930s. [Monroe, Harriet, and Morton Dauwen Zabel, editors. *A Book of Poems for Every Mood*. Illustrated by Janet Laura Scott. Racine, WI: Whitman Publishing Co., 1933]

CHAPTER 34

[Author's collection]

CHAPTER 36

The Dionne Quintuplets, born in 1934, became instant celebrities. Their images were used to sell everything from toothpaste to corn syrup. Here they are posed with Dr. Allan Roy Dafoe, the country doctor who delivered them and became their legal guardian. [Courtesy of N.E.A. Service Inc./Library and Archives Canada/PA-026034]

CHAPTER 37

The University of Minnesota was established shortly after the Civil War in Minneapolis, Minnesota.

CHAPTER 38

This photograph—taken of a corridor at the Triboro Hospital for Tuberculosis in Jamaica, New York—captures the often dark and lonely mood at a sanatorium. [Library of Congress, Prints and Photographs Division, Gottscho-Schleisner Collection, LC-G612-T01-39053]

CHAPTER 42

An illustration by Jessie Wilcox Smith for "The Land of Counterpane," a poem by Robert Louis Stevenson from his book *The Child's Garden of Verses*. Stevenson, author of *Treasure Island* and *Kidnapped* as well, suffered from tuberculosis and spent time "chasing the cure" in Saranac Lake, New York.

AUTHOR'S NOTE

This photo shows girls resting at a tuberculosis sanatorium in Canada. I discovered this photo only after the novel was completed; I almost felt as if it could have been taken of Evvy and the girls at Loon Lake. [Courtesy of the Lung Association of Saskatchewan]

ACKNOWLEDGMENTS

I turned to many sources to learn about tuberculosis and the sanatorium movement. Medical librarians at the University of Rochester School of Medicine, SUNY Upstate Medical University, the University of Buffalo, and the Mayo Clinic helped me gather background materials, as did reference librarians in the Monroe County Library System of Rochester, New York.

To gain a broader understanding of the actual disease and the sanatorium movement, I found three books particularly helpful: Barbara Bates's *Bargaining for Life: A Social History of Tuberculosis, 1876–1938* (Philadelphia: University of Pennsylvania Press, Inc., 1992); Mark Caldwell's *The Last Crusade: The War on Consumption, 1862–1954* (New York: Atheneum, 1988); and *The Forgotten Plague: How the Battle Against Tuberculosis Was Won and Lost* by Frank Ryan, M.D. (Boston: Little, Brown and Company, 1993).

I also read many books written in the 1920s, '30s, and '40s about tuberculosis. These books, though often helpful, tended to focus more on the doctors who worked to fight the disease than on the experience of those who suffered from it. Therefore, I must also thank my friend Jennifer Meagher for introducing me to Theresa Loudin, who spent time in her youth at a sanatorium. Her first-person account, along with those written by Betty MacDonald, Isabel Smith, and others, gave me a richer sense of the day-to-day life sanatorium residents experienced.

Later, when I needed to obtain specific photographs to include in the book, I received help from Michelle Tucker at the Saranac Lake Free Library and from Kelly Stanyon at the Trudeau Institute, both in Saranac Lake, New York, as well as from Renee Ziemer at the Mayo Clinic Historical Unit in Rochester, Minnesota. I must also thank Cynthia Swope, a librarian at the U.S. National Library of Medicine, for helping me check information and locate photos. Librarians at the Library of Congress—especially Gary Johnson—found several key images for the book. Brian Graham, the CEO of the Lung Association of Saskatchewan, assisted me in obtaining the rights to use several images I found on the Canadian Lung Association's invaluable collection of digitized photos (www.lung.ca/tb/index.html), including my favorite picture of the girls "taking the cure" on the balcony of a sanatorium (included in the Author's Note, page 225). I also benefitted from the assistance of the American Lung Association, Urban Remains LLC, and the History Center of Olmsted County, as well as from the generous kindness of the Louis Armstrong Educational Foundation, Inc.

Even with help and insight from such varied and wise sources, any mistakes that I have made in this novel about the treatment and care of patients at tuberculosis sanatoriums are entirely mine.

I could not have made this long journey without the support of fellow writers. My critique partner Linda Sue Park was the first to read a draft of this novel. Her excitement then and through all the many revisions thereafter kept me going when I sometimes found myself running out of breath. So did the wisdom and support of my other critique partners—Vivian Vande Velde, Alice DeLaCroix, MJ Auch, and Jennifer Meagher, as well as Robin Pulver—who stuck with me as the novel slowly took shape. They listened and advised and cheered me on every step of the way. Other writer and illustrator friends—Judy Bradbury, Pam Levine, Cynthia DeFelice, Ellen Stoll Walsh, Donna Farrell, Joan Baier, Dori Chaconas, Lisa Wheeler, Stacy DeKeyser, Shirley Neitzel, and Kelly DiPucchio—as well as everyone in RACWI (Rochester Area Children's Writers and Illustrators) provided support and were all kind enough over the years not to ask, "Haven't you finished that book about girls with TB yet?"

My agent, Tracey Adams (Adams Literary), understands the ups and downs of a writer's life and has been a steady adviser and friend through my good days and bad. She and her husband, Josh, believe in children's literature and care about children's authors—the perfect couple to have in your corner, and they have certainly been in mine.

Many people at Henry Holt and Company have helped with this novel—and I thank them all—but only one person has been at my side from the very start: my editor, Christy Ottaviano. She called to buy my first picture book manuscript many years ago and later bought this, my first novel. She read the original draft, then many other versions, always guiding and nudging me to make big and small changes, to develop my characters, to sort out my story, to find the right word, to revise, revise, and revise. When the manuscript was finally done, we celebrated with another joyful phone call. From that first call to this latest one, Christy has been a valued editor and friend. I will always thank her for believing in me as a writer.

My entire extended family, but especially Marc, Hannah, Lily, Nate, Gretchen, Mary, and Sue, have said the right things at the right times to keep me working on this story. And so have my friends, among them Robin, Risa, Lauren, Susan, Patty, Marsha, Sybille, Kathee, Suzy, Lynne, Sarah, and Judy. I also know that Mayme, Marj, Mrs. Karlson, and Michelle are smiling down with pride to see my finished book. I have learned—along with my characters—how family and friends can ease your sorrow and guide you forward to a new chapter in life. Thanks to all for encouraging me to keep writing the next page.

DISCUSSION QUESTIONS

1. Throughout the story, Evvy makes three 'secret' journeys. What happens on each journey? What does Evvy learn from each experience? What does each reveal about Evvy as a patient? As a friend? As a person?

2. What are Evvy's struggles in her first weeks at Loon Lake? Compare those to her struggles in her final weeks.

3. Compare and contrast the attitudes and care provided by the different nurses, doctors, and hospital staff in the novel. What challenges do they face? Is there one right way to take care of these patients? Why or why not?

4. Compare Evvy's ward mates: Pearl, Beverly, Dena, Sarah. How is each affected by the disease? Does

each girl learn something or change because of her experience at Loon Lake? How does Evvy benefit from knowing each girl?

5. Consider Evvy's relationships with her mother, father, brother, and grandmothers. Do those relationships change over the course of the novel? Why or why not?

6. Though most of the novel is set inside the sanatorium, the outside world is still significant. In what ways? What illustrations connect the reader to the outside world?

7. Consider the importance of gifts in the novel, those Evvy receives and those she gives. Which are the most important and why?

8. What are Evvy's flaws? How do they complicate things for her at Loon Lake Sanatorium? What evidence can you provide that she matures over the course of the novel?

9. What is the significance of Evvy's stuffed bear, Francy, in the story?

10. Which character do you think is most important in helping Evvy survive her experience at Loon Lake? Why?

DID YOU KNOW
TUBERCULOSIS INFLUENCED...

HOW WE DRESSED

People used to have the unfortunate habit of spitting on the ground in public. Because tuberculosis can be spread by the germs found in saliva, women didn't want their skirt hems to touch the ground. As a result, shorter skirts became the fashion.

HOW WE LIVED

In the first half of the 20th century, people were encouraged to sleep with a window open even in cold weather since both the ventilation and the cold air were believed to protect against tuberculosis.

Additionally, many homes were built with sleeping porches, often on the second floor, to allow for maximum ventilation. Next time you drive around a neighborhood with older homes, see if you can spot a screened-in porch.

HOW WE RELAXED

Sitting outside in the sun for long periods of time became a common treatment for TB patients. This treatment—called heliotherapy or phototherapy—soon increased the popularity of sunbathing for healthy people as well. Many of the reclining chairs originally designed for tuberculosis patients soon were favored by sunbathers. Adirondack chairs—with their wide, flat arms for holding books, drinks, or medicines—are still used and enjoyed by people today.

HOW WE ATE

Because patients suffering from tuberculosis often lost their appetites, many people believed that eating a healthy diet, one especially rich in milk and other dairy products, could serve as a defense against the disease. Whereas today we emphasize eating foods low in fat and calories, back then, parents were encouraged to supplement their children's diet to increase the number of calories in each meal.

HOW WE EDUCATED OUR CHILDREN

Schools with special open-air classrooms were built for sickly, undernourished children to attend. Often, walls were removed so the children sat at their desks surrounded by fresh air, no matter how harsh the weather. The schools also had large windows kept open year-round. You can see pictures and learn more about such schools by searching for Open-Air Schools on the Internet or by visiting your own state's historical society.

QUESTIONS FOR THE AUTHOR
MARSHA HAYLES

© G. Schieber

What was your favorite thing about school?

My best friend Julie was an excellent artist, and our teachers in grade school would let us work together on projects. I would write the words and she would illustrate them. Now I know those were really my first picture books. I grew up to be writer and Julie is a professional artist.

When did you realize you wanted to be a writer?

I always liked writing poems and stories. But I never actively submitted my work to a publisher until I took a class on writing for children while I was home raising my own kids.

A piece about a girl on a swing I wrote for that class, eventually—after many, many changes—became my first picture book, *Beach Play*, done with the same editor who worked with me with on *Breathing Room*.

© M. Hayles

Happily writing as a little girl.

What kind of research did you do for this book?

I spent time at libraries of all sorts, especially medical libraries, and visited the Trudeau Institute in Saranac, New York—the town where the sanatorium movement began in the United States. I read fiction books about tuberculosis, memoirs by those who suffered from the disease, and both medical books and articles on the disease. I even came across a sort of crazy picture book called *Huber the Tuber* where the bacteria is turned into a little character.

I also watched a documentary about a sanatorium in Arkansas. In it, former residents told stories about their experiences. I adapted one such account into the events that take place in Chapter 14, "The Giant."

Was there anything particularly interesting you found while doing your research but didn't end up using? If so, what was it?

I learned there is a potentially dangerous side effect to the procedure called pneumothorax, which is something that two of the characters have done in the novel. (See the illustration of a pneumothorax machine before Chapter 21.) If during the procedure, air is accidentally pushed into the bloodstream and travels as a bubble up into the brain, the patient might have seizures, a stroke, or go blind. In an early version of the book, one of the characters did go blind as a result of this procedure. Later I decided that because so many other sad things happen in the story, and tuberculosis can be such an awful disease on its own, I didn't need to add additional heartache to *Breathing Room*.

What challenges do you face in the writing process, and how do you overcome them?

As I was working on *Breathing Room*, I found I was better at keeping track of the places—what things looked like and how they felt—than I was at keeping track of the passage of time. With my editor's help, I needed to settle on how much time elapsed between the many events in the story. I then used the dates on the letters Evvy wrote or received, or the girls' birthdays, or real events such as the news of the Nazis marching into Paris (see the newspaper before Chapter 11) to help establish a timeline of sorts for the reader.

What's the best advice you have ever received about writing?

Whenever my friend and critique partner Linda Sue Park wants me to consider revising a scene, she will say: "Just *play* with this suggestion and see what happens. Don't think of it as work." Who doesn't like to play?

© Vivian Vande Velde

At play with Linda Sue Park

Which of your characters is most like you?

I did model some of my characters on real people, though not necessarily myself. Evvy and her brother Abe, for example, have qualities of my mother and her older brother. Nurse Gunderson with her blond hair, sweet laugh, and kindness reminds me of my dear friend Robin.

Robin, the inspiration for Nurse Gunderson

© M. Hayles

Which characters did you like best?

I would have to say that I had to learn to understand them all, even if I didn't always like them. Although at first Dena seemed sharp and difficult, in time I came to admire her strength and honesty, and she became one of my favorite characters. I also didn't like how controlling Nurse Marshall is and how quick she is to scold the girls, but I know that in her mind she thinks she is doing right by her patients.

Do you ever get writer's block? What do you do to get back on track?

I start and stop writing probably twenty times in a day. I have found that getting up and moving around often allows the words to come to me instead of me trying to chase them down. I start most writing days by walking my dog.

What do you want readers to remember about your books?

I hope they remember Evvy and her friends, and how each girl handles the challenge given her. You don't have to be a superhero to show courage.

What do you consider to be your greatest accomplishment?

Having three great kids comes to mind first. But I am also proud of the fact that I stayed with *Breathing Room* through at least a hundred revisions. I could have quit at any point along the way, but I didn't. I just couldn't let go of my characters until their story was told.

What would you do if you ever stopped writing?

I would probably pursue my musical interests more—and play lots of Scrabble!

What were your hobbies as a kid? What are your hobbies now?

I took ice skating lessons all through my childhood and can still skate backwards, a feat that impressed my own children almost more than anything else I ever did when they were little.

I also played viola all through school and still do sometimes. Finally, my family went fishing nearly every summer. I love to go fishing. Even though I don't actually like to touch or eat fish, I do have a knack for catching them!

What's your favorite childhood memory?

My father had a vegetable garden out in the country, and I would help him plant the corn in the spring and pick it in the summer. Then every year, my parents would host a large corn party for their friends, and I would get to invite a friend over. We would get to eat all the homegrown corn and tomatoes we wanted, plus ice cream and soda, too.

What's your most embarrassing childhood memory?

© M. Hayles

Julie and I playing our instruments.

I played viola for many years in different school orchestras. Once, when we were all crowded onto a very small stage for a con- cert, I was so busy playing that I didn't realize my bow had poked its way into the hair of the girl playing next to me. As I played away, her hair lifted up and down in time to the music.

What did you want to be when you grew up?

I wanted to be a teacher. I played school all the time at home in my basement. I had some old desks, a chalkboard, and various schoolbooks—including some teacher's edi- tions with all the answers (at least that's what I thought). I even turned another room in our house into my school library where I would take my imaginary students to pick out books.

Do you have any strange or funny habits? Did you when you were a kid?

When I was a kid, we had a play ranch set with cowboys and horses and a toy buffalo. Perhaps because of that little plastic buffalo, I have always liked bison. I drive by a buffalo farm not too far from my house and have visited many buffalo reserves over the years. At one such place, I actually got to pet a buffalo and feed it food from my hand.

If you could travel in time, where would you go and what would you do?

I have always wondered what documents were lost when the Library of Alexandria in ancient Egypt burned down. While there, I'd have to pay a visit to a pyramid or two as well.

How did you celebrate publishing your first book?

My family and I took a trip to visit my best friend from childhood, Julie, who had become a professional artist. We bought several of her paintings, which now hang in my house. My kids also got to see some of her art from grade school and finally believed my stories about how talented she was, even as a little girl.

© M. Hayles

Julie and I at an art festival.

What book is on your nightstand now?

I am reading all sorts of books about the Civil War right now, some for adults and some for young people, as I do research for another book.

My messy writing desk.

Where do you write your books?

I have a very nice desk my parents bought me when I was in high school, but it is a little small. I tend to spread out and make a mess of things. For many years, I worked at an old desk of my father's that had drawers that stuck and were hard to open, even back when I was a kid. Now I am using a bigger desk that belonged to my mother. I sit on the same kitchen chair that I used as a child. My desk is by a window so I can look out at the birds and trees in my backyard while I work. Usually, my dog is snoring at my feet.

What do you do on a rainy day?

At camp when I was a kid, we called rainy days cabin days. We would get to stay in our pajamas and read books or play games and take naps. I still love doing all of those things and don't always need a rainy day to enjoy them.

What's your idea of fun?

Getting caught up in a good story whether I am writing or reading it, walking the dog, laughing with friends, playing games with my family, fishing, visiting medical museums,

© M. Hayles

taking trips to see buffalo, swimming, going to Steak 'n Shake (my favorite burger restaurant), listening to music, and traveling to new places.

As a young person, who did you look up to most?

I always looked up to my mother. She was probably the funniest person I've ever known and good at so many things—truly a life-long learner. At ninety she could do more on her laptop than most people my age. She traveled the world over,

My mother at 90, working on her laptop.

and on one trip in her eighties, she chased down a thief who had robbed her and—as she later admitted with some embarrassment—she may even have profited a little from the shakedown.

What's your favorite song?

I listen to music all the time and even put together a playlist of songs for *Breathing Room*. Several songs on that list were written by Leonard Cohen, a singer-songwriter I've admired all my life. Many of his songs are among my favorites.

Who is your favorite fictional character?

Scout from *To Kill a Mockingbird*. She is forthright, honest, stubborn, and curious.

What was your favorite book when you were a kid?

Nancy and Plum by Betty MacDonald, as well as her Mrs. Piggle-Wiggle books.

Do you have a favorite book now?

I like so many books, but *To Kill a Mockingbird* has stood the test of time for me. I especially admire the moment just after the trial ends when Reverend Sykes tells Scout to stand up out of respect for her father. When I used to teach that book, I could not read that passage without crying.

What's your favorite TV show or movie?

When I was the age of my characters in *Breathing Room*, I was a serious fan of Get Smart, a comedy show that parodied spy movies. Back then, there was no way to record a television show to watch again later. So instead I would make an audio tape recording of the program to listen to again and again as I fell asleep at night.

© M. Hayles

If you were stranded on a desert island, who would you want for company?

My kids and my husband since we've been stranded on some long car-trips together and survived!

Stuck on an island together.

If you could travel anywhere in the world, where would you go and what would you do?
I have gotten to travel to many countries, including Australia, Italy, France, England, Scotland, Germany, Spain, Switzerland, Austria, Yugoslavia, Greece, and Canada, but I would love to go on a fishing trip to Alaska sometime. And I've always wanted to visit New Zealand, too.

What do you wish you could do better?
I wish I were neater. But I wouldn't want to be neat if it meant giving up being creative. If given a choice between writing a book or having a clean house, I would pick the book any day—and I have the dust to prove it!

What would your readers be most surprised to learn about you?
That I have an autographed copy of my favorite book *To Kill a Mockingbird*.

© M. Hayles

TO KILL A
Mockingbird

To Marsha Hayles
with best wishes,
Harper Lee

A treasured book.

Check out these
Newbery Honor award-winning books!

Available from Square Fish

The Black Cauldron
Lloyd Alexander
ISBN: 978-0-8050-8049-0

Kneeknock Rise
Natalie Babbitt
ISBN: 978-0-312-37009-1

Abel's Island
William Steig
ISBN: 978-0-312-37143-2

Everything on a Waffle
Polly Horvath
ISBN: 978-0-312-38004-5

The Surrender Tree: Poems of Cuba's Struggle for Freedom
Margarita Engle
ISBN: 978-0-312-60871-2

Joey Pigza Loses Control
Jack Gantos
ISBN: 978-0-312-66101-4

SQUARE
FISH

mackids.com